Heroes of Their Day:
The Reminiscences of Bohdan Panchuk

1 November 1985.
Royal York Hotel
Toronto Ont.

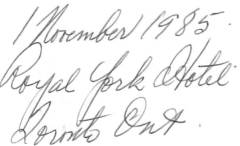

G R B PANCHUK
9061-12TH AVENUE
MONTREAL QUE
H1Z 3J7

This a volume in the MHSO collection
Ethnocultural Voices
General Editor: Robert F. Harney

Publication of this series is a cooperative effort of the
Multicultural History Society and the Ontario
Heritage Foundation.

The Multicultural History Society of Ontario wishes to thank the Ontario Heritage Foundation for its generous assistance in the preparation of this manuscript.

The Ontario Heritage Foundation is an agency of the Ontario Ministry of Citizenship and Culture. Guided by a board of some thirty private citizens, it seeks to foster wider understanding of Ontario's heritage and to stimulate greater public participation in the preservation of the province's historical and natural resources. The Foundation receives and maintains gifts on behalf of the people of Ontario and awards grants for archaeological projects, heritage publications, innovative regional projects and architectural and historical restorations.

The Multicultural History Society of Ontario was established in 1976 with the aid of a grant from Wintario and the Ministry of Culture and Recreation. The Society, an autonomous research institute, works in conjunction with the Archives of Ontario and the province's universities and libraries to encourage preservation of ethnocultural sources and scholarly research about ethnic and immigrant history.

Heroes of Their Day:
The Reminiscences of Bohdan Panchuk

Edited and with an introduction by
Lubomyr Y. Luciuk

The Multicultural History Society
Ontario Heritage Foundation

1983

Canadian Cataloguing in Publication Data
Panchuk, Bohdan, 1914-
  Heroes of their day: the reminiscences of Bohdan Panchuk

(Ethnocultural voices)
Bibliography: p.
ISBN 0-919045-16-2

1. Panchuk, Bohdan, 1914-   2. World War, 1939-1945 — Personal narra-
tives, Canadian.   3. World War, 1939-1945 — Displaced persons.
4. Ukrainians — Europe — History — 20th century.   I. Luciuk, Lubomyr
Y., 1953-   II. Multicultural History Society of Ontario.   III. Title.
IV. Series.

D808.P36 1983   940.53'1503'91791   C83-099207-3

ISBN 0-919045-16-2

Cover photo: Gordon R. Bohdan Panchuk, MBE, CD, 1945

Dedication

I owe much to Father Richard Gregoire, to Alfred McEwan and to Onufrey Klukewich, all from Meacham, Saskatchewan. Without their moral and material support, I would never have been able to complete grades nine through twelve, or Normal School, during those difficult days of the Great Depression. They stood by me, and to these three "heroes" I will forever be thankful.

I was fortunate to have been blessed with an older brother, John, and an older sister, Doris, who often denied themselves the meagre comforts they could have enjoyed in order to give me their hard-earned pennies, which sustained me throughout my schooling.

I can never fully express what I feel towards my widowed mother. She lived only for her children. The father I never knew inspired me to do all that I could for the Ukrainian people. Both of them left me with a legacy which I hope I have at least partially fulfilled.

Most of all I thank Anne, my wife. As club director of the UCSA Services Club, she helped to make that chapter of this reminiscence *our* story, even before we were married. Later she returned to Europe with our relief mission to share the burden of doing all we could to save the displaced. She knows best what we faced together in those days and since, and she has had to put up with the most. No man could have been more fortunate in having a helper and partner as faithful and devoted as she. Without her, this memoir would never have seen the light of day.

G.R.B.P.

Contents

Preface

Ethnocultural Voices is a collection of reasonably priced publications, including memoirs, diaries, autobiographies, reminiscences and other sources which contribute to our understanding of the immigrant and ethnic experience in Ontario.

The series is a joint effort of the Multicultural History Society of Ontario and the Ontario Heritage Foundation and reflects our commitment to increase public awareness of the diverse origins and past of Ontario's people, encourage scholarly study of ethnocultural history and foster an ethos of multiculturalism among Ontarians of every origin and background.

At first glance, Bohdan Panchuk's story does not seem relevant to Ontario's history. He was born and raised in the Ukrainian communities of the western Prairies and spent most of his active career working in Montreal and Great Britain on behalf of Ukrainian refugees and Canadian Ukrainian organizations. However, it was Bohdan Panchuk, more than any other Canadian Ukrainian, who alerted his countrymen to the plight of their fellows in Europe. Thousands of Ontarians of Ukrainian descent and their children who read these reminiscences will gain new insight into the initiatives and agencies which brought them to our province. Others will understand how Panchuk and his friends turned their sense of ethnic solidarity and of humanity into deeds which saved many DPs from repatriation to the Soviet Union.

Despite the imperatives of ethnic fellow feeling and humanitarianism, both the Canadian Ukrainian rescue effort and the attempts of the Ukrainian refugees to organize their own future were beset by factionalism and the misunderstandings which naturally arise among people who share ethnicity but not a common history. The jungle of agencies, political movements, umbrella organizations and their accompanying acronyms divide Canadian Ukrainians less today than they once did, but they should be seen not just as reflecting conflict but as a sign of the vitality and commitment to survival of the ethnic group. Catholic, Orthodox and leftist free thinker, Canadian and European, men and women from East Ukraine or from Galicia, Bukovina and the Carpathians, *Waffen* ss men and Allied soldiers — it was within such a welter of conflicting Ukrainian sub-identities and loyalties that Bohdan Panchuk and his friends worked to save lives, reconstitute families, bring refugees to Canada and find the networks of aid and goodwill which might forge a new Canadian Ukrainian identity. The task was formidable and neither all the Canadian Ukrainian leadership nor those among the DPS who saw themselves as emigrés, or as part of a nation in exile, shared his approach. Panchuk's reminiscences then are his own.

Others who took an active role in the rescue effort, many of them mentioned in these pages, should be interviewed, their thoughts and memories recorded. Only from such a total effort to reconstitute the past will historians in the future be able to understand this important phase of Canadian and Ukrainian history. Often when a memoirist gives his version of forgotten events, there is little documentary material preserved to say him nay or to confirm his interpretation. That is not so in this case. The Panchuk reminiscences appear in conjunction with the donation of his massive collection of archival and historical materials about the period to the Multicultural History Society of Ontario for deposit in the Archives of Ontario.

Lubomyr Luciuk, the interviewer of Mr. Panchuk and editor with him of the tape transcripts, is completing a doctoral dissertation in Human Geography at the University of Alberta. He is himself an expert on the wave of Ukrainian immigration covered by these reminiscences and knows the documentation in the Panchuk collection. He has provided the necessary gloss to the text, but has wisely let the author speak for himself.

Robert F. Harney

Introduction

World War Two precipitated fundamental geopolitical realignments in Europe, which left in their wake just over thirty million people uprooted and displaced from their homelands. Specialized international agencies were formed, even before hostilities ended, to cope with this emerging refugee problem. One of the first was the United Nations Relief and Rehabilitation Administration (UNRRA). Its mandate included providing the Displaced Persons (DPS) with foodstuffs, shelter and other emergency supplies, while working in tandem with those military and occupation administrations being set up in the ruins of the Third Reich whose purpose it was to ensure an orderly removal of these refugees back to their countries of origin. At the time it was routinely assumed that repatriating these DPS was the only viable solution to the immense refugee problem, that indeed this option was even in keeping with the wishes of the people themselves.

Yet, the root causes of any refugee phenomenon are always of a political nature. UNRRA soon found itself entangled in complex debates over the fate of those DPS who were unwilling to return to their homelands. In accord with the terms of the Yalta Agreement, the Soviet Union and its eastern European satellites demanded that all persons they claimed as their citizens be returned, regardless of the personal aspirations of the individuals concerned. Most Western countries, informed by their humane tradition of asylum, suggested that those refusing repatriation to their areas of origin be offered the prospect of emigration to whatever countries of resettlement became available.

While the protagonists worked out their differences of interpretation, in the immediate postwar years of 1945, 1946 and even into early 1947, hundreds of thousands of DPS and political refugees suffered the tragic fate of being forcibly repatriated to the USSR. Eventually, with the establishment of the International Refugee Organization (IRO) in July 1947, these involuntary popula-

13

tion transfers declined. Resettlement became the more common solution to the remaining refugee problem, and so, by mid-1947, thousands of DPs were journeying overseas, to North and South America and any other lands willing to accept them.

Within the overall DP population of postwar Europe, one estimate placed the total number of Ukrainians at some two million people. Al least thirty to forty thousand of these were eventually allowed to settle in Canada. They came from all regions of Ukraine, a land which, prior to 1939, had been dismembered, then occupied by four powers—Soviet Russia, Poland, Romania and Hungary. Most Ukrainians in the DP camps carried passports or other identity documents which formally assigned them citizenship status in one of these four states—or else they were labelled ''Stateless'' or ''Unknown.'' The Ukrainians made it clear, however, that they wanted to be described and treated as Ukrainians. What were the UNRRA and later the IRO teams to do with a people whose identity and area of origin were debatable—no matter what the Ukrainian DPs might themselves claim—and whose existence as a nation Western governments were rather reluctant to recognize? For officialdom the matter grew more complicated when it became increasingly clear that few of those describing themselves as Ukrainians were willing to return voluntarily to territories under Soviet hegemony. Since there were likely more Ukrainians within the overall refugee population in Europe than any other ethnic group, the question of determining who these Ukrainians were, what they wanted and what could be done with them took on considerable importance.

Fortuitously for the Ukrainian DPs and political refugees, there had been some forty thousand Canadian Ukrainians in the Canadian armed forces during World War Two. They had demonstrated their loyalty to a country where there had been those who doubted it, so now they demanded to be heard in the council chambers of the West whenever issues having to do with Ukraine arose. Since many of them had encountered Ukrainian DPs even before the war ended, i.e., Mr. Panchuk on the beaches of Normandy, they were well aware of the scale and importance of the Ukrainian refugee problem, and were not about to ignore it. Publicly, they insisted that these people were ideal immigrants whom Western countries should welcome with open arms as settlers of the best

14

possible quality. Privately, they hoped that an influx of Ukrainian DPs would strengthen the somewhat precarious existence of organized Ukrainian life in countries like Canada. So motivated, these Canadians began their own refugee relief and resettlement operations. By presenting the official authorities with a *fait accompli* they were able to avoid the censure that such private initiatives might otherwise have met.

One of the most prominent of these Canadian Ukrainian servicemen was Gordon Richard Bohdan Panchuk. The son of Ukrainian pioneers to Canada, this hardworking and dedicated activist within the ranks of the Ukrainian Orthodox church movement had been a teacher in rural Saskatchewan before the war. He had volunteered for service shortly after the outbreak of war in 1939. Once posted to the United Kingdom, he established contact with the small colony of Ukrainians in Manchester, around whose Ukrainian Social Club he helped form the Ukrainian Canadian Servicemen's Association (UCSA). Its London club at 218 Sussex Gardens became something of a home away from home for the thousands of Canadian Ukrainian servicemen who were posted overseas. Subsequently—although not without some friction developing—Mr. Panchuk used this UCSA core to create a new organization, the Central Ukrainian Relief Bureau (CURB), which by late 1945 had initiated its refugee relief operations on the Continent. Later it would be complimented by the Canadian Relief Mission for Ukrainian Refugees (CRM)—together the two were pivotal in ameliorating the often desperate situation in which some Ukrainian DPs found themselves.

The story of Mr. Panchuk's efforts overseas occupies most of the account which follows. This is neither Mr. Panchuk's autobiography, nor is it a complete story of Canadian Ukrainian refugee relief work. Only certain episodes and events have been recalled, providing a skeletal outline of what occurred during these momentous years. It must be emphasized that this is Mr. Panchuk's interpretation of these events—different perspectives would most likely be forthcoming from others active in the effort, such as Stanley Frolick, Ann Crapleve, Anthony Yaremovich and Anne Wasylyshen. The immediate postwar years were turbulent and there were contentious moments—some of these have been all but forgotten, others have yet to be forgiven. It is to Mr. Panchuk's credit that he has not attempted to avoid discussing these problems, for by so doing he has provided grist for many scholars' mills. Very possibly the publication of this, his own views on the immediate postwar period, will prompt some of the others involved in those events to offer their own descriptions. If this occurs, the present book will have accomplished much for Canadian Ukrainian history.

What follows are the edited transcripts of interviews I held with Mr. Panchuk over the past three years, during the course of my doctoral research. Since these reminiscences are largely self-explanatory, only brief and occasional footnotes have been added. I have not altered Mr. Panchuk's version of the events here described even when my own research has led me to different conclusions. The selection of documents and photographs was done with a view to illustrating some of the activities Mr. Panchuk refers to, while adding substance to his assertions.

These recollections serve at least one further purpose. Mr. Panchuk, aware of the fact that may students of the Canadian Ukrainian experience have been hampered in their inquiries because of the inaccessibility of primary source materials, entered into an agreement with the Multicultural History Society of Ontario in December 1980. Through the good offices of this organization, he arranged to have his voluminous private collection of archival material—memoranda, reports, correspondence, organizational records and minutes of meetings, photographs, even film—transferred to the Archives of Ontario in Toronto. A preliminary finding aid for this, "The Gordon R. Bohdan Panchuk Collection," was prepared in October 1982 by Messrs. Jurij Serhijczuk and Zenowij Zwarycz. Scholars are likely to discover that this archival material constitutes one of the most significant deposits of material pertaining to the Ukrainian DP experience in existence.

Following the May 29, 1946 meeting of the Senate Standing Committee on Immigration and Labour, the Canadian government decided to alter its policy and allow Ukrainian DPs to immigrate into this country. Dr. Vladimir Kaye (Kisilewsky), a prominent Canadian Ukrainian historian, wrote to his friend, Tracy Philipps (an enigmatic Englishman who did much to force the creation of a Ukrainian Canadian Committee in 1940) that Mr. Panchuk's role in prompting this change had earned him the right to be considered "the hero of the day." When Mr. Panchuk was reminded of this letter, he immediately insisted that such praise was not for him alone—that it befitted *all* those Canadian Ukrainians who tried to help the Ukrainian DPs, both during and after World War Two. From that observation came the title for this book.

A few words of gratitude. My original contact with Mr. Panchuk came through Mrs. Rozalia Charitoniuk of Kingston, Ontario. When she first mentioned Mr. Panchuk to me, I had little idea of what his role in Canadian Ukrainian history had been. After I met him, and many of the others who had been involved in CURB, CRM and affiliated groups, it became apparent that a major episode in Canadian Ukrainian history had been all but ignored.

Many others helped see this project through to completion. I wish to thank: Andriy Bandera, Bill Daly, Mr. T. Danyliw, Mr. S.W. Frolick, QC, Dr. O. Fundak, Dr. Michael Kapusta, Professor Leszek Kosinski, Miss Helen Kozicky, Martin LaVoie, Jacques and Debbie Litalien, Dr. Michael Lucyk, Dr. Manoly Lupul, Dave Mason, Bernie and Margaret Mullen, Stephen Pawluk, General Joseph Romanow, George Salsky, Rev. S. Sawchuk, Mrs. Ann Smith, BEM, Dr. Peter Smylski, Megan Stephenson, Mrs. Anne Wasylyshen, Anthony Yaremovich and Stephan Yaworsky.

I would also like to thank Professor Robert F. Harney of the Multicultural History Society of Ontario, who originally urged me to pursue this effort; Anne McCarthy, the Society's associate editor, who brought order to my interview transcripts; and Yurij Luhovy, who assisted in preparing the photographic material. My own support was provided for by a Social Sciences and Humanities Research Council of Canada Doctoral Fellowship and the Samuel P. Woloshyn Memorial Award from the St. John's Institute in Edmonton.

Finally, I wish to thank Mr. and Mrs. Panchuk. It is fitting that the son of two Ukrainian refugees of the post-World War Two years should have played a small role in helping Mr. Panchuk tell his story. I hope that by doing so I have given him an indication of the thanks that many undoubtedly feel is due him for his labours and dedication.

Lubomyr Y. Luciuk
Doctoral Candidate
University of Alberta

17

Abbreviations

AUGB	Association of Ukrainians in Great Britain
AUUC	Association of United Ukrainian Canadians
BUC	Brotherhood of Ukrainian Catholics
CCG	Control Commission for Germany
CRM	Canadian Relief Mission for Ukrainian Refugees (also known as Canadian Relief Mission for Ukrainian Victims of War)
CURB	Central Ukrainian Relief Bureau
CUYA	Canadian Ukrainian Youth Association
Dyviziia Halychyna	The Ukrainian Division "Galicia"
EVW	European Volunteer Worker
FUGB	Federation of Ukrainians in Great Britain
IGCR	Intergovernmental Committee on Refugees
IRO	International Refugee Organization
LVU	Canadian League for the Liberation of Ukraine
ODUM	Organization of Democratic Ukrainian Youth
OUN	Organization of Ukrainian Nationalists
OUNr	Organization of Ukrainian Nationalists—Revolutionaries (also known as the *Banderivtsi*, or followers of the OUN of Ste pan Bandera)
OUNs	Organization of Ukrainian Nationalists—Solidarists (also known as the *Melnykivtsi*, or followers of the OUN of Col. A. Melnyk)
PCIRO	Preparatory Commission for the International Refugee Organization
Plast	Ukrainian Youth Association—Plast
SEP	Surrendered Enemy Personnel
SHAEF	Supreme Headquarters Allied Expeditionary Force
SUM	Ukrainian Youth Association
SUZERO	Ukrainian Association of Victims of Russian Communist Terror
UCC	Ukrainian Canadian Committee
UCRF	Ukrainian Canadian Relief Fund
UCSA	Ukrainian Canadian Servicemen's Association
UCVA	Ukrainian Canadian Veterans' Association

UCYO	Ukrainian Catholic Youth Organization
UHO	United Hetman Organization (also known as the *Hetmantsi*)
UHVR	Supreme Ukrainian Liberation Council
ULFTA	Ukrainian Labour and Farmer Temple Association (later AUUC)
UNDO	Ukrainian National Democratic Alliance
UNF	Ukrainian National Federation
UNRRA	United Nations Relief and Rehabilitation Administration
UNRada	Ukrainian National Council
UPA	Ukrainian Insurgent Army
URDP	Ukrainian Revolutionary Democratic Party
USRL	Ukrainian Self Reliance League
UUARC	United Ukrainian American Relief Committee
UWL	Ukrainian Workers' League
UWVA	Ukrainian War Veterans' Association
YUN	Young Ukrainian Nationalists (later Ukrainian National Youth Federation)
WBA	Workers' Benevolent Association

Reminiscences

The Roots of My Involvement

My story really begins with my father Michael Panchuk. He was born in 1862 in Torhowytsia, a village in the Horodenka area of West Ukraine. I never really knew him. He died on June 24, 1915—less than five months after I was born—of asthma I think. My mother's maiden name was Maria Bowkowa. Both of them emigrated to Canada before World War One—he in 1913, she in 1914. He came here first to establish a homestead, build a little hut for his wife and children. After he made a little money he sent it back to them so that they could join him in Saskatchewan—my mother, my elder brother John and my elder sister Doris (she was the oldest in the family). They came to Canada in the fall of 1914, just prior to the outbreak of the war.

My father meant to farm here, but he was never really a farmer. He was an intellectual. He was the kind of person who studied and supported Mychajlo Drahomanow[1] and Ivan Franko[2] and their teachings and philosophies. He was involved with the radical movement which had dedicated itself to the cultural and intellectual revival of Ukraine. In fact, it is probably true to say that he came here only because he could not continue working for this cause in Ukraine. He could continue it here. He took a homestead near Peterson, Saskatchewan because that was the best way of establishing himself as a citizen of Canada. But, to be honest, he was never a farmer, nor did he really have much of a chance

---

1. Professor Mychajlo Drahomanow, born September 6, 1841, was a Ukrainian publicist and a leading member of the socialist movement.
2. Ivan Franko, publicist and Ukrainian activist, was a founding member of the Ukrainian Radical Party in 1891.

to become one here. He was an educated man, for that period of time, one of those who had been in the SITCH in West Ukraine. As I say, his efforts were all dedicated towards trying to improve the lot of the Ukrainian people in the homeland. The SITCH movement was headed by Dr. Kyrylo Trylowsky.[1] It was my father's example that later inspired me to do all I could for the Ukrainian cause.

My mother was uneducated. She could neither read nor write. (Up until her death, she still signed her name with her mark +.) Spiritually, however, she was totally devoted to my father. He did all he could to teach and inspire her to learn more. She learned parts from Ukrainian plays and operas that she could not read but that he taught her. She certainly tried hard to educate herself in Canada, and she used us, her children, to help her. She did a wonderful job educating herself and us and instilling in us respect for education.

Two children came with my mother to Canada. I was born after they arrived, and five months after my birth my father died. It was a hard life in Saskatchewan, and my mother had to make ends meet somehow. She had to run the family, she now had three children to care for. Somehow or other—I'm not aware of the details—she was contacted, or she met a man who had come from a neighbouring village in western Ukraine—John Badyk from Toporiwtsi, not far from where my parents were born and reared. So my mother re-married—in common law since there were no priests or churches at that time in our part of Saskatchewan. Badyk was alone, she was alone—and so they came together in common law. As a result of that, we had two brothers and two sisters added to our family. There were four Badyks—Anne, Fred, William (Bill) and the last, Pauline. As far as we were concerned, they were blood relations, and we got along very well as one family, and still do. For a while they became Panchuks, but as grew up they wanted to revert back to Badyk. And we agreed with them. So now when I visit my brother, Bill, or Fred, I'm a Panchuk, and they're Badyks, but we are brothers.

---

1. Dr. Kyrylo Trylowsky founded the paramilitary SITCH organization in 1900, which formed a core around which Ukrainian military forces were built up during World War One. He was also a correspondent for *Svoboda* (Freedom). He died in 1941.

John Badyk was also a farmer. He moved from his first homestead in the Colonsay area to another right next to ours. A time came when he and my mother couldn't see eye-to-eye. So each had their own farm there in Saskatchewan, side by side. We had my father's original homestead—the registration of which was transferred to my mother—so when they separated, my mother had a place of her own to go to. The children went with her. My stepfather was killed in an accident about 1936, kicked to death by a horse. So my half-brothers and half-sisters know almost as little of their father as I know of my own. Again my mother was left a widow, only now with seven children, carrying the load for both husbands. Somehow she made do. She died on December 5, 1956 and was buried in Saskatoon.

As for religion, well, my father was probably an agnostic. Originally in the old country, both my parents were Greek Catholics (Uniate), but they had become radical already in West Ukraine. My mother less so because she was not literate. Both tended to accept the "anti-clerical" stance taken by the radicals of that period. When they first came to Canada the strongest religious group in that part of Saskatchewan was the Independant Orthodox Church movement.[1] The farm my stepfather bought next to ours was originally settled by Reverend Zazulak, one of that church's ministers. In fact, their first church was to have been built on our farm, but because of registration difficulties and delays, it was built on a neighbouring farm, now owned by John Polischuk, next to where the first cemetery was, now abandoned. (That is where both my father, Michael Panchuk, and my stepfather are buried.) Of course, there was also a tremendously strong Protestant missionary drive among Ukrainians, right across Canada, especially in western Canada. They set up all kinds of first institutions—churches, schools and community centres—supposedly to salvage Christian and cultural lives. Some Ukrainians resisted them. They felt this drive was assimilating them too much.

---

1. Bishop Seraphim organized an Independent Orthodox Church in Canada in 1903, with the aid of the Presbyterians. His activities were considered to be tendentious within Ukrainian church circles in Canada.

Our Area

My district in Saskatchewan was almost entirely Ukrainian, although by convention and conviction there were different types or subgroups within this Ukrainian population. Differences among them developed further as time went on. In the beginning though, when Ukrainians first started settling in Canada after 1891, they took the first piece of land that was available, as long as it was the closest to a brother, a sister, or an aunt, or some relative. That was the way people settled. All they wanted to do was be close to a neighbour who was also Ukrainian and, if possible, from the same village. That's all they wanted.

The first thing that I recall was, of course, going to school. My eldest sister took me to school. I didn't have any idea what to expect. And the name of the school was "Drahomanow." Now why that school was named Drahomanow, I didn't know until much later. I don't think my sister knew either. Likely my father had a say in that. Our community of Ukrainians appreciated the three great intellectual leaders of the Ukrainian cultural movement of that time, namely, Drahomanow, Franko and Shevchenko. In every home, wherever they could, people hung pictures of Drahomanow, Franko and Shevchenko,[1] ans they were followers of one or the other, or all three. As a result the small Ukrainian communities in Saskatchewan came together and built schools and community halls and named them Shevchenko, Franko, or Drahomanow. Or course, in some locations such halls, community centres, or schools were also named after the villages or areas of Ukraine from which the locals came. The buildings and their names reflected these people's Ukrainian commitment. How intense these national feelings were, how deep the ideological differences among them were, I can't really recall. We children knew that on one weekend we would be going to the Franko Hall, on the next weekend to the Shevchenko Hall and on the next weekend to the Drahomanow School for a concert. But the ideological programs for Ukrainians, represented by each name, were beyond us.

---

1. Taras Shevchenko (1814-61), known as the "bard of Ukraine," was a poet, writer and painter whose patriotic insights helped revive Ukrainian national aspirations during the late nineteenth century.

24

I became aware of some of the differences early though, as a child of ten or twelve years, driving to a concert organized in memory of Shevchenko, naturally being held in the Shevchenko Hall. We went by horse-drawn bob-sled. We attended a dance after that—my father and mother were not around, so I went with my brother and sister. We went on our own, played it by ear, enjoyed what was good and reflected negatively on what was bad.

The differences between the three groups are hard to present now. The Shevchenko people—and this, incidentally, is also reflected in eastern Canada, such as in Montreal where they also had Shevchenko, Franko and Drahomanow societies—were patriotic supporters of the idea of an independent Ukraine. The Franko group was likely semi-socialist radical. The Drahomanow group was more socialistic and inclined to see a federal relationship with Russia. Those people who believed that society belongs to everybody followed the Drahomanow group. There was no strong religious connection to these things. If anything, and this is putting it mildly, the Shevchenko were more religious—either Ukrainian Orthodox or Catholic—while the radicals were agnostic, and the Drahomanow group was probably disinterested in religious questions.

The local Drahomanow School I attended had been organized by Ukrainian settlers in 1911, and they insisted that when they got their permit from the government, they would run the show. So it was that the school was run by them. I do not think there has ever been a teacher in the Drahomanow School who was not a Ukrainian. All teaching was in English during regular hours, but there was extra Ukrainian-language teaching after hours. "After four" they called it. Of course, it was a regular, official Saskatchewan Department of Education school. And the teachers had to do their instruction in English or be reprimanded. But the school board insisted that, if a teacher was hired, he would have to do Ukrainian instruction after hours. In our school then there were no non-Ukrainians. So the teacher had to be fluent in Ukrainian. It was about the only way he could communicate. He would often have to speak in Ukrainian even while giving an official lesson, just to get a point across. One teacher I remember was Paul Syraishka, another was Andrew G. Pawlik, who still resides in Winnipeg and is now president of the Trident Publishing Company, which publishes *Ukrainski Holos* (Ukrainian Voice) and *Kanadiiskyi Farmer* (Canadian Farmer). He was my teacher when I was in grade six. There were many others, all of whom I don't now recall except for N.F. Calmuskey, C. Nowalkowsky and Michael Stolabisky. Teachers often changed every few months. So that in 1926, for instance, we had three different teachers, the last being Mr. Pawlik.

There was no outside world for us. Our own world was very closed—it was the only one we knew. We were so removed! This was the early twenties—our world was Ukrainian. We did what we did in our own way, in the way we felt like doing it. We were all the same, basically one single Ukrainian community, joined together by the bonds of national identity and especially by a shared language. We lived Ukrainian. We played ball and hockey and cheered in Ukrainian. The language kept us together more than anything else. We sang folk-songs together we had all learned in the same language, and during the holidays we sang Christmas or Easter carols. Everything we did in daily life was permeated with this sense of being Ukrainian, even though we were living in Canada.

The outside, non-Ukrainian world crept in only in the mid 1930s when such newspapers as the *Winnipeg Free Press*, the *Prairie Farmer*, the *Western Producer* and the Eaton's and Simpson's catalogues became more commonly available; those, in effect, became the "bibles" for the people who could read English. That is when we really became more fully aware that there was an outside world that was very different from our own. We, the young people, read the letters to the editor published in these papers, and especially the comic strips, also in such papers as the *Chicago Herald* and *Tribune and Examiner*. Our parents didn't care. So as far as we were concerned—as I was—the comic strips, letters ans short stories were the most interesting. There were no radios around at that time in our area. I was a teenager when I listened to my first crystal set. Most of the news we already got from Ukrainian newspapers. In our area, at that time, the majority read *Ukrainski Holos,* perhaps before that *Kanadiiskyi Farmer.* After that there were two or three publications put out by the Ukrainian communists in Winnipeg—*Farmerske Zhyttia* (Farmer's Life), *Robitnychi Visti* (Worker's News) and *Robitnytsia* (Female Worker) came regularly. The first two were weekly newspapers and the women's magazine was a monthly. They must have been free, for I never recall our family paying subscriptions. We were much too poor to be able to subscribe to any kind of newspaper. These left-wing publications were the most common in our area without any doubt. The local people were mostly peasants, farmers and workers, and they were mostly leftist. I think that if things had gone differently, if my father had lived, he would have moved farther in that direction, towards the left-wing in Canadian Ukrainian politics. I had an uncle, Ivan Panchuk, in Saskatoon whom I met ten or fifteen years afterwards when I went to Normal School there, and he was as left as you can make them.

At the time there were no regular Ukrainian church services in our area because there were no churches. (Our neighbour, Reverend Zazulak of the Independent Orthodox Church, christened me. The church itself lasted only a few years. It was sold by the lumber yard owner in Dana to pay the debt on the lumber the people bought on credit to build the church.) There were only irregular Protestant, I think they were Methodist, sermons given by occasional itinerant missionaries. No Ukrainian Orthodox or Catholic churches existed—one would have to look into our church history in Canada. There were a few followers of Bishop Seraphim around; there seemed to be so many movements after the souls of people then, it is now impossible to analyse them all. But certainly, in our case, there was no national Ukrainian church. Up until I left high school I had never been inside a church.

In my rural area it depended on whose neighbour you were whether you called yourself a Ruthenian or Ukrainian.[1] Our next-door neighbour, Polischuk, came from East Ukraine. The family considered themselves closer to the Russian ethnic group than we did. We felt more akin to the people of the Carpathian Mountains, the Hutsul mountaineers. So when we would meet the Polischuks, which happened almost every day, we were convinced that they were Muscovites or Russians, while they considered us Hutsuls.

---

1. The term "Ruthenian" was commonly used before World War One to denote Ukrainians. The latter appellation became more common after the appearance of *Ukrainski Holos,* published in Winnipeg from 1910.

In these interwar years, there were few of us in the community who had done enough reading and thinking about nationality; most were, after all, illiterate. People only gradually coalesced under the name Ukrainian. As we grew up, so did this Ukrainian consciousness.

I have gone back to my home town since the war, and many of the people are still as parochial and obstinant as their parents were when I was growing up there. One of my contemporaries later became the principal of the Drahomanow School, but nothing changed. He's still there. Intermarriages occurred and helped to iron out what differences there were and make people more conscious of their common Ukrainian identity. But, you see, the tragedy of Canada and of our Ukrainian cause here was that many of our people left the rural districts and moved into the cities. We lost most of our roots on the land. As this happened, the bloc settlements disappeared and with them the social, cultural and economic bases of our Ukrainian way of life here. The new urban environment where most Ukrainians now live is so different from that in which I was raised. Now, of course, everyone is conscious of being a Ukrainian—no one calls himself a Ruthenian anymore. Yet I wonder what effect there will be in the long run on Ukrainians in Canada who no longer live side by side, bur are dispersed throughout the cities? Our Ukrainian landscape in Canada is all but gone now.

School Days

I went to school eight miles south of Meacham, Drahomanow School, District #2501. It was in the year 1928, roughly, when I left grade six. Grades seven and eight were senior grades, but by that time my sister Doris was working as a maid in a hotel in Saskatoon. She took me to the city and shared her quarters with me. So I did grades seven and eight there. I went to the Princess Alexandra School, a public city school. My sister also arranged for me to take violin lessons. We all learned to play various instruments and had our own family orchestra. The Ukrainians there were by far in a minority, only two or three per cent. In the country schools we were well prepared, so I went through both grades in one year. I wasn't too shocked by the switch from rural to urban living, although it was a completely different environment. I was always a dreamer. I just took it in my stride.

After finishing both grades I went back home. My sister had her own life and couldn't keep me. She was the adult of the family and helped by sending money back home. Our family was being run by my mother, aided by my elder sister Doris and, to some extent, by my brother John. So I went back to the farm. But they were convinced that I should keep on going to school. We all couldn't go. We couldn't afford it. I was chosen to continue with my schooling. The family decided on this. They made arrangements for me to go to school in Meacham. It was the only place to go, being the nearest high school. So I did my post-elementary in Meacham High School—grades nine, ten and eleven. My teacher throughout those years was Mr. Bert Walsh. He taught all four grades (eight to eleven), averaging a total of about twenty to thirty students.

We survived away from the farm by working at anything and through the help of other people, living wherever we could. We did all sorts of things. It was very difficult during the Great Depression, but we coped as best we could. In the summers my brother John and I went out to work, cutting bush, building highways, shooting gophers. There was a seven-cent bounty for each rodent destroyed, you had to bring in the tail as proof. We hunted crows and collected their eggs. The bounty on crows was two cents an egg, or five cents a leg. So you would wait for the eggs to hatch, then sell their new-born legs to get the extra amount. We collected empty beer bottles along Highway 2, which ran past our farm, and sold them for five cents each. You did anything you could because it was the only way to get the money to get the coal-oil to keep the house lamps lit, or buy sugar for the kitchen table and contribute to the flour that my mother would have to buy once a month to keep bread in the house.

No one else of the elders in my family really went to school much beyond the seventh grade. My older brother went as far as grade seven; my older sister got to grade five. Of my two younger half-brothers and -sisters, two finished high school, and one of these, Anne, became a school teacher with our help. Actually that was already mostly with my help. When I had become a school teacher myself, I helped the rest of the family get along.

29

My last year at Meacham High School was the hardest. I just couldn't find a place to live for free, and we had no money to pay for accommodation. During my three high school years here, I lived in about fifteen to twenty homes—in attics, back rooms, usually sharing a bed with some boy in the family—a few months here and a few months there, at the Dupchaks', the Konovaletz', the Klukewichs' and including one spring and autumn on the floor in an abandoned shack on the Meacham nuisance grounds (where all the garbage was dumped on the edge of the salt lake). My family would bring me enough food for a week which I ate cold, a bit at a time, until I finished it or it spoiled. There was no stove and no washroom there. I washed and had water to drink when I got to school where I went early and stayed as long as possible. I spent the longest time with Father Richard Gregoire at the vicarage. The deal was that my brother John would bring the priests firewood for the winter if they would keep me. Meacham was a prairie town and our homestead was on the edge of the wood belt. Ukrainian farmers from the Meacham area used to come to our place during the winter, cut their firewood—which we sold to them at three to seven dollars a load on the stump. When Father Richard was moved by his bishop to Saskatoon, he arranged for me to remain in the vicarage, and I lived for a while with Fathers Mulcahy, Jolly, Lemaire and Ash—rectors of St. Edward's Roman Catholic Church. I was "inherited" by each, like the furniture. I lived with the priests and worked with Mr. McEwan in his lumber yard.

After finishing grade eleven in Meacham in 1931, I went back to Saskatoon. To get there my mother and I travelled by horse and buggy. I'll always remember that trip, travelling during the day and sleeping in the open fields by the side of the road at night. It took us four days to get to Saskatoon so that we could make arrangements for me to take my grade twelve there. Grade twelve was not offered in Meacham. But during grades nine, ten and eleven, I had made friends with people in Meacham. One of them, at that time, was a most important citizen in Meacham—a town of about 150-200 or so people—the manager of the local lumber yard, Mr. Alfred E. McEwan for whom I had worked. He had moved to Saskatoon where he became the proofreader for the *Saskatoon Star Phoenix*. Because he was there and we had already become friends in Meacham, I had decided that I could count on his help to put me through grade twelve.

When my mother and I got to Saskatoon, she went to her friends to sleep overnight, and she did her business and I did mine. I went to the McEwans' to see if I could live with them free of charge if I came back to do grade twelve. I really had no place to sleep over that night, and I was too proud to ask the McEwans if I could spend the night with them, so I went back to the livery barn where we had stabled our horse. But the barn was locked so I crawled into the cylinder of an old steam engine where I spent half the night. It was cold and windy, and about two or three o'clock I had to get out and walk around. But I was scared the police would arrest me for prowling as a horse thief, so I sneaked into the railway yard where there were many boxcars. One was slightly open and seemed to be half full of sawdust. I crawled in and went to sleep on the sawdust, which proved to have blocks of ice under it. I nearly froze!

The McEwans agreed to my boarding with them while at school if I would be willing to help wash the floors, clean the dishes and the like, which I was. And that's how I went to grade twelve and eventually to Normal School, living both years with the McEwans. I had an oral agreement with the McEwans that once I got my first teaching job, I would repay them, at $25 per month, for all the time I had lived with them during my schooling, 1932-33, at grade twelve, and 1934-35 at Normal School, which was a teacher-training school, the nearest road to employment and earning money so I could start paying back my debts and helping my family. I took a year off in between 1933 and 1935 and worked for Mr. Onufrey Klukewich, who owned a garage service station and hardware store in Meacham, in order to make enough money to go to Normal School. I was eighteen then. I slept in a little cubby storage room where he kept oil drums. There was just room enough for a cot and a chair. I used the public town toilet and fed myself. During harvest I went out stooking and threshing with local farmers—Klukewich's friends whom he conned into hiring me as "a good young boy who is trying hard to go to school and get ahead on his own because his mother is a widow and has a large family to feed." I never properly repaid in cash my debts to Father Richard, Mr. McEwan, or Mr. Klukewich, but later during

World War Two and after, I did what they would have liked to have done and what I am sure they expected me to do.

While in Saskatoon I couldn't keep away from organized Ukrainian community life. Since childhood, my mother, more than anybody else, had imbued us children with a sense of being Ukrainians—this was our link with the past, you might say, with my own father's beliefs and efforts. All the time — from grades nine to eleven—I would dream about the day I would get involved in Ukrainian community activity and do something. My mother was very conscious of the fact that we should be involved. So even while living with the McEwan family, I became an activist for the Ukrainian youth movement. We had a choir at the Normal School, and I helped to run it. I worked with Ukrainian students living at the P. Mohyla Institute, since the majority of the Ukrainian students at the Normal School were from the institute.[1]

Organizational Ties

More by accident, I think, than by choice, I became involved with the Ukrainian Self Reliance League (USRL). I was exposed to other Canadian Ukrainian organizations, such as the Ukrainian Labour Farmer Temple Association (ULFTA) and also slightly to the Ukrainian National Federation (UNF). The oldest, strongest and most established political and cultural groups active among Ukrainians in the early twenties were the ULFTA—a socialist and pro-Soviet movement now known as the Association of United Ukrainian Canadians (AUUC)—and the pro-Canadian, democratic Ukrainian Self Reliance League—which became closely aligned with the Ukrainian Orthodox Church of Canada.[2] The Ukrainian Catholics were slowly getting organized around their parishes, but were slower in getting active in cultural work. The Ukrainian National Federation, most of whose members were Ukrainian Catholics, was a post-World War One creation organized by vet-

---

1. The Petro Mohyla Institute, established in Saskatoon in 1915, was the cradle of the Ukrainian Greek Orthodox Church in Canada, and an educational and social centre for the affiliated secular movement which became the Ukrainian Self Reliance League.
2. For a history of this church, see Paul Yuzyk's *The Ukrainian Greek Orthodox Church in Canada, 1918-1951* (University of Ottawa Press, 1981).

erans from the Ukrainian armies of the liberation struggle, 1917-21.[1] The UNF was founded in 1932 in Edmonton although the real roots go back to Saskatoon and the formation of its predecessor, in 1929, the Ukrainian War Veterans' Association (Ukrainska Striletska Hromada). Saskatoon was also the birthplace of their newspaper *Nouyi Shliakh* (New Pathway) and for many years was th seat of their headquarters. The UNF was incorporated in 1950.

I was aware of these various groups, but by choice I accepted the tenets of the USRL. I felt closer to it probably because of my involvement with the P. Mohyla Institute. My elder brother had also attended the institute when he was in grade seven, for half a year, while I was a junior still in grade five. He didn't finish the year because we had no money to pay for his keep there. The Saskatchewan teachers who taught at Drahomanow and neighbouring schools were invariably from the Mohyla Institute. It was really a force in the early years of Canadian Ukrainian life. That attracted me. The Orthodox movement was patriotic yet new. It would change the lives of our people in Canada for the better, I felt sure of that.

So I joined the Self Reliance League and the Ukrainian Orthodox Church of Canada—both founded more or less at the same time. It was all part of the growing segmentation and polarization of the Ukrainian community in Canada, brought about in part by the move to cities and by a new post-World War One immigration which brought in new ideas regarding Ukraine. If anything, it was more by our mother's design, I think, that we children went in that direction. She was illiterate, but she had great intuition. That's why she sent my brother to the Mohyla Institute. She sold her last cow to send him there. She had an instinct which none of us at that time could fully appreciate. My connections with the Ukrainian Orthodox church I should also credit to my mother. Certainly, it was because of her that I went to high school in Meacham where I began my connections with the Orthodox and USRL movements.

The general policy of USRL was, and is, that we should not belittle the needs of Ukraine, or the aspirations of the Ukrainians

---

1. For material on the 1917-21 Ukrainian liberation struggle, see Taras Hunczak, *The Ukraine, 1917-1921. A Study in Revolution* (Harvard Ukrainian Research Institute, 1977).

in the old country. Indeed we should do everything we can to help, *but* we can do most as Canadian citizens—as citizens of an already established country which has its own interests and intellectual influences. This would ensure that we were not treated as "enemy aliens" in the event of some international conflagration, as happened during World War One here in Canada, when there were thousands of Ukrainians interned because of their suspected disloyalty to Canada.[1] And I think that this is where we differed most from the other Ukrainian organizations here—while we felt we should be devoted to helping solve the Ukrainian problem of lacking an independent homeland, we kept maintaining that the only way to serve it was, first of all, to be good Canadians. By being a loyal Canadian, we said, you could influence other Canadians and the Canadian government into policies supporting the liberation of Ukraine, which we all believed was necessary. But you cannot do it on a tangent all on your own. And I think that this is what inspired our generation, at least my circle, of young Canadians. We had to be Canadians first, *good* Canadians first, and only after everyone else appreciated this could we also act as good Ukrainians. Lord Tweedsmuir, who was Governor General of Canada at the time, used just such an idea when he spoke before an audience in Frazerwood, Manitoba in 1936. And that idea inspired many of us. To be a good Canadian, be a good Ukrainian. Both could be combined and worked out together. We have consistently tried to do so.

I Start My Teaching Career

I finished Normal School in June 1935, went back to Meacham and started looking for a job as a teacher. Mr. Klukewich said, "Well, I'm going to help you get a job." He's the man who, after I had made many applications, drove me down to Yellow Creek and delivered me to the school there in September 1935. They had accepted my application. He told the school board, "I'm bringing

---

1. For analyses of the Canadian internment operations 1914-20, see L. Luciuk, "Internal Security and an Ethnic Minority: the Ukrainians and Internment Operations in Canada, 1914-1920," *Signum* (Journal of Royal Military College of Canada) IV, no. 3; and Francis Swyripa and John H. Thompson, eds., *Loyalties in Conflict* (University of Alberta Press, 1983).

you a young student who'll be your teacher. He has no money. Give him everything he needs to have on credit. If he doesn't pay for something, I'll take care of it.'' That was his commitment. I was left there to teach—my first real job—and he went home. I signed a contract that my salary would be the government grant—whatever it was. The first year's grant was $350, I believe. And that's what I accepted, thanks to Klukewich. They could only pay me once a year, after the people harvested and paid their taxes, after which the provincial government gave each school district its grant for education.

To be honest, I wasn't really equipped to teach anything. All I could teach was how to be a good human being. I had scratched the surface of history, mathematics, English and so on—at high school level. I could keep ahead of the students. But in a serious sense Normal School had only just equipped us with the rudiments for teaching. We were glorified baby-sitters. But in Ukrainian cultural terms, we had a little more background in music, choir, folk-dancing (all self-taught), and the people wanted that more than anything else. They weren't interested in the academic side of school as much as what you were going to do with the children after school and on the weekends. The government prescribed what was taught between 9 a.m. and 4 p.m., after 4 p.m. it was expected that we'd dedicate ourselves to Ukrainian work.

The first school I got had fifty-two students from kindergarten to grade eleven inclusive, and all in a one-room schoolhouse. I had to teach all the students and all the classes by myself at the same time. Almost all students were Ukrainian, at least 99 per cent. I think there was one Hungarian there. I was twenty years old. There were few people my age in that local area. I had succeeded a teacher, Mrs. Wasyl Cherewick, who was older and possibly more capable than I and whose husband was already doing his Ph.D. for the Department of Agriculture, University of Manitoba. They were living there in the teacherage. I claimed the residence when I accepted the contract, but I agreed that they could live with me as long as they wanted. I didn't need the whole two-room house, so they stayed for three or four months while they looked for another place. They eventually went back to Winnipeg, and I think she stopped teaching. I took over the district.

Yellow Creek was a community looking for leadership, for someone to take it out of the "wilderness." The inhabitants were still pioneers. Many of them had originally settled in Manitoba, and, in some cases, the same people, or their eldest sons, took new homesteads now in Yellow Creek. In this sense they were all pioneers for a second time. Anyway, they were looking for direction. The public school teacher had to provide it. I just happened to fit the bill, I suppose. My age made no difference to them at all. They just wanted someone to tell them where to stand, where to sit, when to do this or that—assign the pitch, alto, soprano and so on. I taught the small children normal hours, then after hours the adult community. And the children had to put on a concert almost every weekend, and we had to produce something on nearly every commemorative occasion you can imagine—in memory of Taras Shevchenko, Mother's Day, and so on—for everything the community wanted. If you didn't produce these theatrical and cultural events, then you weren't a good citizen or a good teacher.

There was really little or nothing else for the people, culturally speaking, in Yellow Creek. The community was empty—a vacuum. As it turned out, the majority of people eventually went Orthodox. But at the time, there were as many Ukrainian or Uniate Catholics as Orthodox. I think there was even a Ukrainian Catholic church founded there a year or two before the Orthodox one. There were two church parishes. The Catholic priest was Father Ryshytylo. He lived with me in my house every time he came to the community (two or three times a year), as did the Orthodox priest, Father Mayba. A teacherage had room to put up the priest. None of the farmers had enough spare room. So, either priest made his home with the local teacher. When we put on a Ukrainian concert, it was a joint effort—a community effort—and nobody questioned the religion, or affiliation, or anything, of the performers as long as they spoke Ukrainian and could sing a song or two. That's the way it was. And, at that time, there were no Ukrainian communists of the ULFTA in the Yellow Creek area at all. Of course, I had had some contacts with people in the ULFTA during my school days, but I don't think I had real friends there. It was mostly older people, ten or twenty years older than I was, who belonged to it. I was a member of USRL, in particular, its Canadian Ukrainian

36

Youth Association (CUYA). It is probably the first and oldest Ukrainian youth organization in Canada. (In 1981 it celebrated its fiftieth anniversary.) We had a very good CUYA group in Yellow Creek in the late 1930s. We travelled around giving concerts and so on.

I was a teacher in Yellow Creek from 1935-39. I can recall when I had my first inspector's report as a teacher, the inspector was a strong WASP who wrote that I was a wonderful teacher, but: a) I spoke with an accent which was non-British, and b) I devoted too much time to affairs which were not Canadian—that was his point of view. The secretary of our school board showed me that report and said, "Well, let him go fly a kite! We want you. As long as you're happy, we want you here." Outwardly, I didn't let it seem to bother me too much. In my heart, it burnt me up. I was doing more for the empire and for Canada than he was; he was an inspector of schools, driving around in his car. I could not even afford one, and I was teaching young children which I thought was good. I thought I was doing a little bit more than he was. Later I and thousands of other Canadian Ukrainians made sure that these people knew that we were conscious of the fact that they didn't trust us and suspected our loyalty to Canada. We enlisted *en masse* during World War Two—relatively more than any other ethnic group in Canada. Did they contribute to the same extent that we did? But that inspector's report is one instance that helped move me to do some of the things I did—you know, this annoyance that somebody thought he was more Canadian, or more British that I was, when I thought that I was as Canadian or British as anybody else was. And I experienced this feeling back in Normal School when I was becoming a teacher. When we had a big world map spread out showing the British Empire, I felt that we too were part of it, a big thing.

I Volunteer

I could have stayed on in Yellow Creek for the rest of my life. I suppose I would have enjoyed it. They wanted me to stay, except that by nature I didn't want to when there was a war on. When war broke out on September 1, 1939, I volunteered. I submitted my application to the RCAF, and the school board went looking for a replacement. In three years the school had grown from one classroom of eleven grades to four classrooms of many students with three teachers in addition to myself. I was the principal by then, with my senior experience. The board hired another teacher, Miss Ann Hawrysh, who had a B.A. Technically, she and I felt that she should be principal for she was ahead of me in education, even if junior in experience. So we had a final arrangement where I said that once I resigned they'd obviously appoint her as principal. It was a very friendly arrangement. I resigned and she took over and became principal. I went to Saskatoon to prepare for my forces training and while waiting for the call-up enrolled at the University of Saskatchewan in an arts program while also taking part in the campus Canadian Officer Training Corps (COTC).

When I was in the COTC in 1939, the second in command there was Captain John Charnetski, a Ukrainian. I didn't realise at the time that a Ukrainian could ever get as far as being a commissioned officer. Here was I—just enrolled, a cadet, fresh from the farm, from Yellow Creek—and here was John Charnetski, second in command of the COTC at the University of Saskatchewan. Hey, I thought, we're getting places, you know! That impressed me.

When I moved to Saskatoon, I bought a little house there for around $370—a little shack with no running water or indoor bathroom. I completed one year of my arts course and COTC, but only finished a few months of my second when I was called up. So I dropped out and went into training for the services. I chose the air force. I wasn't interested in anything but Air Crew, but I didn't qualify because I had weak eyes. But there was a special training program—the Dominion Provincial Youth Training Program—that took people like me and gave us background training (mostly wireless and electronics) for other fields than Air Crew. I went into wireless operations—a special course which lasted almost a year in the Saskatoon Technical Collegiate Institute. They gave us training in radio operation, repairs and the like. While we were being taught, we received a basic wage from the government. At that time I was living in my own home at 1307 Alexandra Avenue and was also the director of the cultural program at the P. Mohyla Institute and at the Ukrainian National Home. So almost every day I had work to do among Ukrainian youth—all this over and above my military technical training. In addition I taught Ukrainian school in the Ukrainian National Home on Avenue I, which was connected with the Orthodox parish in Saskatoon, and I was a CUYA instructor for their Branch No. 1 in Saskatoon. We had about fifty people, with a choir, a dancing group, an orchestra, an amateur theatre and all kinds of activities. We were CUYA, and only as that were we involved in the Ukrainian Self Reliance League (USRL). When I was leaving for overseas, they put on a farewell party for me in the Avenue I Ukrainian hall and presented me with a leather suitcase and a gold ring with the CUYA Trident pin mounted on it. I still have them. To me they are tokens of reward and inspiration.

My mother was both happy and sad when she learned of my enlistment. She was happy that I was doing what I wanted to do, but a little bit disappointed in that she was counting on me to carry her through. But we settled that very amicably. I made a commitment that when I joined up she would get half of my service pay—whatever I got from the RCAF. That gave her the security that she needed. So she moved into my little shack in Saskatoon, and for the duration of the war she got her allowance (half my pay), was secure and thought that her son had done reasonably well providing for her. My elder sister, Doris, also went into military service for a little while, then she joined the National War Services working in the dockyards. But she couldn't help maintain my mother. My older brother was married by then and so he had a wife to look after. He was also in the service for a few months. So, from the point of view of mother's security, I had to provide it and did. Both my half-brothers and half-sisters also enlisted for longer or shorter periods. All seven of us served in the forces in one form or another and for various periods of time, but I alone served for the duration and overseas

Canadian Ukrainians and the Ukrainian Question in Europe

The USRL didn't have real political connections with the Ukrainian nationalist groups in Europe. Colonel Evhen Konovalets visited Canada in 1928.[1] He wanted to mobilize the Ukrainians in Canada

---

1. Colonel Evhen Konovalets was a member of the Ukrainian Military Organization and, after 1929, the leader of the Organization of Ukrainian Nationalists. He was assassinated in Rotterdam by a Soviet agent on May 23, 1938.

to support the Ukrainian Military Organization, which later became the Organization of Ukrainian Nationalists (OUN). He spent many months living at the P. Mohyla Institute. During this time he had meetings with people like Wasyl Swystun, the Stechisin brothers and others in the community. They tried to work out an arrangement whereby USRL would support the Ukrainian nationalists in the old country financially, morally and materially. The stand of USRL was, "We'll do it. We're willing to do it because we're all for it. But it has to be done openly and legally, through a bank account. We want accounting. We want receipts for monies spent. We want acknowledgements for monies received and so on. We want to know where and how the money we collect and give to the movement is spent." Konovalets rejected this approach. OUN was an underground movement; it just could not publicize its logistical bases. So Konovalets didn't reach any accord with the USRL. Instead OUN came to rely on the Ukrainian National Federation, or rather its core group, the Ukrainian War Veterans' Association.

Konovalets took a logical attitude, given his plans and the realities of Europe, but it wasn't logical to our pioneers. They were so indoctrinated with the attitude that for everything they did they wanted a piece of paper, receipts, a document, something to show proper accounting for their hard earned funds. No arrangement with Konovalets could be made. Of course, the financial aspect was not the only problem. There were other ideological and philosophical differences which influenced the USRL leaders. They didn't want to be seen as part of some European political organization, lest these ties appear suspect to the Canadian government. Don't forget, Ukrainians in Canada had endured several years of internment operations in this country during and just after World War One because many of them were registered as Austrians. Then they had been suspected of having dubious overseas sympathies and loyalties and were considered enemy aliens. Who among the USRL leaders would willingly risk bringing down on his organization's members more of this type of treatment?

There was another movement here in Canada that aligned behind Hetman Pavlo Skoropadsky, living in Berlin. During 1937-38 his son Danylo toured the United States and Canada, visiting Ukrainian communities in order to mobilize support for this conservative, royalist movement. He was living in England and remained there throughout World War Two. When the younger Skoropadsky made his trip to Canada, the same thing happened as with Konovalets. The different community leaders met, they talked, but they didn't come to any logical conclusion. So when war broke out in 1939, both the Skoropadsky supporters and the OUN were already working on their own plans to support the struggle in Ukraine. They had covert and open links to their movements there that did make them suspect in Canada, and I am sure they must have been monitored by the Canadian government.

In talking of Konovalets' and Skoropadsky's visits, I would say that they succeeded in only 25 30 per cent of what they wanted to do here. The majority of Ukrainians in Canada were not going to be involved in either movement. But two very serious events did take place in Ukraine in the thirties—the "Pacification" in western Ukraine (1930), initiated by the Poles against Ukrainian aspirations for autonomy, and the artifically induced Great Famine 1932-33, which decimated the Ukrainian population subjugated by the Soviets. Over seven million people were starved to death by Stalin. Both events deeply touched Canadian Ukrainians spiritually and emotionally. We had demonstrations, sent protest petitions to Ottawa, delegations, and collected relief funds. Our elders were very much concerned, but most of our youth were indifferent. The masses just wanted to be Canadian, to be left alone; whatever side Canada chose, they would be on that side. Oh, they hoped, perhaps even dreamed, that Canada would always be on the side of Ukraine, Ukrainian independence, the struggle for freedom and so on.

Maybe one in a hundred of my age group in western Canada even knew about OUN, that they had a network of their own, with propaganda offices in Geneva, Berlin and London. If one in a hundred did know, it would still be irrelevant. The average Ukrainian Canadian in my generation just didn't care about what was happening in Europe that much. We accepted the British Empire, we accepted that every Christmas we would have a message from the monarch. We accepted the fact that our flag was the Union Jack, that our mother country was Britain and the empire, even though it may be wrong to feel this way. I think even my mother—and this is hindsight now—if faced with the problem of deciding whether she should be for Canada or Ukraine, would say, "Well, Canada gave us bread and butter. We'll stick by Canada." I have that suspicion.

Still, to go back to Ukrainian politics for a moment, my feeling about the accusations against Konovalets and Skoropadsky as being pro-German is that these were unfounded rumours. Both of them were patriotic Ukrainians, just as good as I was, or anybody else. They, like others, were just looking for a means to free Ukraine. What relations they had with the Germans before World War Two were based more on expediency and hope than on any pro-German convictions. They were certainly *never* fascists, or pro-Nazi. This was my feeling. I was convinced that neither Konovalets, nor Skoropadsky, both of whom had been in Canada and gone back to Europe, was any less Ukrainian than I was. In fact, I'd say there wasn't that much difference.

One of the plans that their supporters came forward with in Canada, which was very logical and sensible, was *to train young people*. So they established military schools, even flying schools like the UNF's in Oshawa, and more. Both UNF and the United Hetman Organization (the *Hetmantsi*) are still very proud of their efforts, claiming that they helped train people who then fought for the benefit of Canada; although they weren't really thinking of Canada's war needs as much as how they could help Ukraine. And I think that these training courses they offered helped them recruit new members for their own organizations. You know, when you went out to Alberta, Manitoba, or Saskatchewan and said, "We're helping Canada in the war, and we have a flying school in Oshawa"—well, that attracted recruits. Later these same young people, from the youth organizations—YUN (Young Ukrainian Nationalists), UCYO (Ukrainian Catholic Youth Organization) and CUYA—rallied behind the Canadian war effort, and many volunteered for duty. The ULFTA's people, until 1941, didn't support Canada—they were pro-Stalin, then allied with Hitler.

Let me explain, in 1939 the ULFTA, following Soviet party thinking, approved of the Molotov-Ribbentrop Non-Aggression Pact between Nazi Germany and Soviet Russia.[1] So they did

---

1. For a discussion of the ULFTA, see John Kolasky, *The Shattered Illusion: the History of Ukrainian Pro-Communist Organizations in Canada* (Toronto: Peter Martin Associates, 1979).

everything possible to agitate against Ukrainian Canadians volunteering for Canadian military duty. We volunteered because we felt we should defend Canada. We were aware of the fact that there was agitation against joining, but we knew our duty and were loyal. The majority of the Ukrainian Canadians (say 75 per cent) who joined the armed forces in the period 1939-June 1941 were either directly involved, or, at least influenced by the three main Ukrainian youth organizations of the time (CUYA, UCYO and YUN). Take, for example, the fact that Peter Worobetz, Joe Romanow and I, all of whom are veterans, were each from one of these organizations (CUYO, YUN, CUYA respectively), which provided most of the Ukrainian Canadian youth for the armed forces—directly or indirectly. One of the effects was that returning veterans were much more interested and became involved in Canadian affairs, especially politics. The first Ukrainian Canadians to be appointed to the Senate (W. Wall-Liberal and P. Yuzyk-Conservative) were veterans. Many veterans joined the Canadian civil service after the war, Ukrainian professional and businessmen's clubs sprang up all across the country, in most cases founded or spearheaded by veterans.

Of course, there was dissent within the ULFTA over the Molotov-Ribbentrop deal. It was demanding quite a lot of these people to make them accept this 1939 partnership between Hitler and Stalin. Dissent arose just as in 1935 when they had fragmented over the question of the Great Famine of 1932-33 and Russian behaviour in Ukrainian territories under Soviet rule. As far as the Canadian authorities were concerned now, the ULFTA's stand was one that placed them in the enemy camp. If the pact hadn't been made, I don't think I would ever have been as antagonistic to the Ukrainian national communist movement, if you can call it that. But this alliance with Hitler, I thought that was going too far. And so to me, personally, when the Canadian government confiscated and closed down the ULFTA halls in 1940, well good for them! It served them right! Some of these halls were sold to patriotic Ukrainian *Canadian* organizations, for example, in Saskatoon the USRL got one, and in Toronto the UNF; in other places, other organizations or church parishes took advantage. From the point of view of our USRL movement—and even from that of the Ukrainian

Catholics—I think it was good that it happened because many of these befuddled older Ukrainian communists were so disenchanted that they came around to our way of thinking and joined our organizations, became readers of our newspapers and so on. Possibly, for Canada it was a good thing also. It helped break the left.

Then on June 22, 1941 when Germany invaded the USSR, the ULFTA had no alternative but again to switch, now to jump on the bandwagon, crying "We're on the same side! Down with Hitler!" It was an interesting metamorphosis. To date, all history being taught in the USSR claims that World War Two (The Great Patriotic War) is dated from 1941-45, not 1939-45. Later, once we had organized our Ukrainian Canadian Servicemen's Association (UCSA) Club in England, one of the fifteen or twenty founding members was from the ULFTA crowd in Winnipeg. He was just as diligent about scrubbing the floors, washing the dishes and doing everything we needed done in the club as anyone else because we were now on the same side. Quite a few of these leftists joined us in London and became ardent in their support of UCSA and its club.

Going Overseas

My preparatory military training in Saskatoon to be a wireless electrical mechanic was not very long—about six months with pay but still as a civilian. I had a few months in RCAF basic training at No. 1 Manning Depot in Toronto (where, in our off hours, some of us helped out with the CUYA branch at St. Vladimir's Ukrainian Orthodox Church, 404 Bathurst Street). There then followed almost a year at RCAF No. 1 Wireless School in Montreal (Queen Mary Road) where I first graduated as a wireless operator ground (WOG) aircraftsman first class (AC1), remustered as a wireless electrical mechanic (WEM), was promoted to leading aircraftsman (LAC) and in December 1941 was posted overseas.

We went overseas on the SS *Stratheden*, spending three or four days in Bournemouth, England before being posted to Ireland. There were all together about fifteen Canadians posted to Ireland and attached to the RAF. Three of us were Ukrainians. There was Steve Kalin, who joined us in Toronto, a school teacher from Krydor, Saskatchewan; Walter Weslowski, originally from

Ukraina, Manitoba; and myself. We were on the same ship going overseas. (While in Montreal at No. 1 Wireless School there were four of us Ukrainian Canadians who stuck together all the time, training together and visiting the CUYA together at St. Sophie Ukrainian Orthodox Church on De Lorimer Avenue, when off duty: Steve Kalin; John Magus, another school teacher from Hafford, Saskatchewan; Max Strilchuk, a high school graduate from Arran, Saskatchewan; and myself. Of the four, Steve Kalin and I were posted overseas upon graduation. Max Strilchuk and John Magus were posted to RCAF units in Canada. Max got an overseas posting later. John never got overseas. Walter Weslowski did No. 1 Wireless School in Montreal before us, but was on the same overseas draft as Steve Kalin and I, and we met for the first time on the ss *Stratheden*.) As far as I know, Steve, Walter and myself were the only three Ukrainian Canadians stationed in Ulster, and the three of us toured—hitch-hiked—around the country in our off-duty time. In a way, we were the founders of the Ukrainian Canadian Servicemen's Association (UCSA) because it was then that the idea for the association was born (later formally founded on January 7, 1943 in Manchester, England).

We wanted to have a club for cultural and social reasons. We wanted to be able to meet at Ukrainian Christmas and Easter. How else could we do it overseas? We had met other Ukrainians in the forces and become friends in Montreal while in training at the No. 1 Wireless School. We also had friends in Toronto at the Manning Depot, and we had friends who had gone into other branches of the Canadian armed forces. We knew this was a very important time in Ukrainian affairs—after all, independent Ukrainian states had been formed between 1917-21. There were many of us in the service. Since Kalin, Weslowski and myself were all CUYA members, we realised we would have to get youth from other organizations, other Ukrainians, involved. So we said, "Somehow or other we have to do something about getting all Ukrainian Canadians together, regardless of what their affiliations might have been in Canada." Soldiers have to stick together to be effective.

Up until then I had been writing a regular weekly column for *Ukrainski Holos* called "CUYA Pathway." As a teached I had lots of CUYA experience as an organizer in the years prior to enlistment

45

(1935-40). From 1935-41 I used every moment of my free time (weekends, holidays, summer vacations) organizing CUYA branches and jamborees in Saskatchewan. There is hardly a district or community that I didn't visit in the province. As a result, I had an extensive circle of friends, many of whom were also joining up. It seemed a most natural thing to get them organized *again,* once in the forces, to promote common cultural and social ends and interests. So, already on the *Stratheden* the three of us decided that something should be done. We made a pact then that we'd keep in touch, that we'd maintain contact all the time, never let it drop. And the other thing we decided was who was "Joe." I was to be Joe, responsible for taking the initiative. In Ireland Walter Weslowski got stuck with servicing seaplanes flying trans-Atlantic missions. Steve and I were with Spitfires—radar (VHF) work. But we kept in touch all the time, and we got together whenever we could to do all kinds of things. I established and maintained a large correspondence with Ukrainians in Canada and gradually with those who joined the forces and were posted overseas. But there was no Ukrainian community there in Ulster.

Discovering the Ukrainians of Manchester

In the meantime, however, we found out about Ukrainians living in Manchester in England, and each of us tried to plan a holiday in Britain where we would somehow or other get in touch with them. We eventually—all three—got posted to Britain. I think I was the first of us three to contact the Ukrainian community in Manchester. But other Ukrainian Canadians had already visited there. One of them was Michael Cannon (Kalyniuk) from Hamilton. We had not heard of him before, none of us. But he got in touch with the Manchester Ukrainian community and even married the daughter of one of the community members—Olga Lesniowsky, daughter of Joseph Lesniowsky, the secretary of the Ukrainian Social Club at 188 Cheetham Hill Road, Manchester. Another Ukrainian Canadian from Hamilton, in the First Canadian Division to go overseas, was Harry Sluzar. He also married in Manchester. Shortly after he was killed at Dieppe.

The Ukrainians in Manchester were there by accident. They were originally coming to Canada from Ukraine and got stuck there. When we met them we found that they were people completely devoted to the Ukrainian cause and happy to see Canadian Ukrainians. Prior to the war little was known in Canada, if anything, about this small Manchester Ukrainian community. There were some fifteen to twenty families living a very insular social and cultural life centred around their Ukrainian Social Club. Without this community, there might have been no Ukrainian Canadian Servicemen's Association (UCSA). They provided us with our first "home away from home." For them we provided a window to the outside world. Their greatest contribution to our association at the beginning was providing premises and people (two girls, Olga Lesniowsky and Pauline Tarnowski) who volunteered to look after our first UCSA office there.

Creating the Ukrainian Canadian Servicemen's Association

UCSA was formally constituted in Manchester, January 7, 1943. I still have the original minutes of our first meeting as recorded by the late Alex Kreptul, at that time elected as our first secretary. We published the story of "How It Began" in our first promotional booklet, *UCSA*, October 1943, when I was already stationed in Digby, Lincolnshire. That's where the booklet was designed, written and printed. I doubt if any copies can now be found. Nearly forty Canadians attended this first founding Get-Together from all across Canada, between Montreal and Edmonton. They are all listed in the UCSA booklet, as are the names and addresses of the Ukrainian families in Manchester who hosted us. Apart from constituting the organization itself and drafting its terms of reference and future plans and direction, a resolution was made there and then to hold the second Get-Together at Easter. In the interim everybody had homework to do—gather more names and addresses, write home to their respective parents, friends, organizations, or parishes and submit all gathered material on potential members to myself, Corporal B. Panchuk, the elected president. Others on the elected executive were Steve Kalin, Walter Weslowski; Michael Turansky (a YUN and UNF supporter from Saskatoon) became vice president, and soon after we recruited Helen Kozicky (a UHO follower from Calgary) as secretary. We had to have a broad representation. We even had a few people from the Polish forces—F/O George Salsky, F/L Serhij Nahnybida and F/O Michael Oparenko—people who were involved with us, but who

47

were not eligible for executive posts because UCSA was intended to be a strictly Canadian affair. These men, at that time, were there only as observers. We welcomed them as that, but we wanted to underscore the point that as Canadians and members of the empire, we were forming this new group, UCSA. We wouldn't allow any of the Polish forces to have any say in our doings. We were going to do it our way.

Things were happening so fast during the war, you just could not appreciate the difference between a normal, civilian operation and war. War moved so quickly. Things happened daily that normally took years. I became a regular and frequent visitor to Manchester and became involved with the community as a teacher at their Ukrainian school, which I founded. As I was in the service, the only time I could teach was on the weekends when I wasn't on duty. I had to take the train to Manchester from Digby. But at that time none of these disadvantages mattered to any of us. As long as we could keep things going, do Ukrainian work, we felt everything was fine. I would sleep on the train, or board with one of the Ukrainians in Manchester, teach the children reading and writing in Ukrainian, singing and music—we had a choir and a mandolin orchestra much as in Yellow Creek before the war. We were then preparing a Mother's Day concert to be held at the Easter Get-Together. They were so happy to have me as a frequent visitor to Manchester that they made me president of their local Ukrainian Social Club.

The second UCSA Get-Together was held in Manchester at Easter, May 2, 1943, as planned, and solidly confirmed the operation of UCSA at a general meeting held in the school of St. Chad's Church. Over seventy-five servicemen attended, more than half of whom were new members. Another booklet was compiled and published covering the proceedings of this second Get-Together. Among the decisions made here were two basic progress ones—to hold the next Get-Together as soon as possible in London and to start looking for premises for a club of our own in London.

By the time the Mother's Day meeting was held, we had already culled our own service records (at various stations and orderly rooms), and any name that we considered to be Ukrianian, we put on our cardex system. I also wrote and had published in the Ukrainian-language newspapers in Canada a number of press releases appealing to Ukrainian Canadian fathers and mothers to send us names and addresses of their sons and daughters stationed in Great Britain. The response was terrific. In a few months we had over 1,000 names and addresses. As a result, we had sent out invitations to them for this May Second meeting. We didn't know who these people were, all we had were names, units and regimental numbers. Many were from the three Ukrainian youth organizations I have named, but many were ex-ULFTA, ULFTA and just young Ukrainians never before affiliated.

Among the most ardent was Andrij Nykoluk. He had been leftist ex-ULFTA originally from Winnipeg, later Toronto. He was elderly but a terrific fellow (later a key organizer for our first Rome Get-Together). All the people we had represented a broad cross-section of Ukrainians from Canada, completely impartially organized. It had nothing to do with numbers of people in Canada. It was all based on the initiative of these people themselves in response to our appeals in the Canadian Ukrainian press and through UCSA circular letter and newsletter. We were too young to be disturbed by the community factionalism that was so characteristic of interwar Canadian Ukrainian life. Our second secretary, Helen Kozicky, was a supporter of the Hetman movement. Nobody then even knew or cared. To have a nationalist from UNF, a member of UHO and a Catholic operating alongside people from USRL and the Orthodox groups was really unheard of before we started UCSA. The war was the thing that linked us together—the uniform, the Canadian badges, the camaraderie of men and women in wartime. At our first Get-Together in Manchester our Canadianism created such a bond that half the time we didn't know who the other guy was, but we didn't care too much. Only afterwards did we often find out where people came from or fitted in, their past background, or their affiliations, if any. Back in Canada by November 1940, the war had also brought all Ukrainians together, and a united Ukrainian Canadian Committee (UCC) was formed to support the war effort. It soon achieved a harmonious spirit of cooperation, which we had first managed to develop in UCSA. UCSA had provided UCC with a reason to exist. Ours was a really unique and genuine unity; in our Canadian Ukrainian history I doubt if you can find such inter-organizational cooperation before, or, for that matter, since.

49

At our first meeting we had also had present Lieutenant John Swystun. He was the first commissioned officer to come to UCSA. We were so proud of him that we put him right on top of our list of elected club officers, in the executive without election. All these first people in UCSA were just "buck privates" scrubbing floors, peeling potatoes, doing all the lowly jobs, but they were all good people. John V. Swystun was the son of Wasyl Swystun, one of the founders of USRL and one of those who had helped establish the Ukrainian Orthodox church in Canada. He would later switch to supporting UNF, and from then further left to supporting AUUC. John Swystun, his son, had helped to bring in many more commissioned officers to UCSA. By October we had about a dozen members who were commissioned officers. When the war ended UCSA had between 500 and 1,000 commissioned officers. Two of our early UCSA members reached the rank of brigadier-general—Romanow and Andrunyk.

The Ukrainian Canadian Committee's Role

As I've said, the UCC had just barely organized at that time; their first Congress wasn't held until June 22-24, 1943 in Winnipeg. And they were very weak in those early years. They did massively support our UCSA Club in London for the whole time we were operating. That was one of their greatest contributions to the war effort. Bringing the UCC together was no easy matter. Non-Ukrainians played a major role. Professors George Simpson and Watson Kirkconnell were very involved—as was the rather mysterious Tracy Philipps, whom Lord Halifax, the British foreign secretary, apparently sent over to Canada—in the founding of Ukrainian Canadian organizations.[1] There was a third element,

---

1. Tracy Philipps had this to say about the formation of the Ukrainian Canadian Committee:

   Unification of New Canadians and elimination of their discords. In constructive diplomacy as in bone ailments there are two main methods. The first method is the most spectacular, prompt and popular. It often requires other operations to follow. It is rapid, drastic and aggressive. One attacks the foreign element which has entered the body politic. In the realm of diplomacy it takes the form of threat and direct action. It is a regrettable wartime technique extended to the realm of the civilian. This, in effect, is the only method which, in the time allowed, could be used to unite the

however, the common cause of the Ukrainians themselves, namely that we have got to stick together whatever happens. There was a war to be won, after all.

Before UCC was formed between November 7-9, 1940 in Winnipeg, there were two Canadian Ukrainian committees, the Central and the Representative. The basic difference was political. One, the Central, was formed out of members of UHO, USRL and Ukrainian Workers' League (UWL); the other, the Representative, of people from UNF and the Brotherhood of Ukrainian Catholics (BUC).[1] The UNF was then considered to be pro-German, as were the Hetman followers. The others—USRL, UWL, BUC—were not suspect insofar as the Canadian authorities were concerned. Only after 1941 did their anti-Soviet sentiments arouse some official worry. My own commission in the RCAF was delayed because I had spoken up somewhere in the barracks against the USSR—at that time our ally.

Tracy Philipps had a major role in the formation of UCC and later helped us with UCSA and CURB.[2] He was *persona grata* in official Canadian circles and in Britain. I think the fact that he was married to a Ukrainian, the pianist Lubka Kolassa, and had

---

half dozen discordant groups of Ukrainians in Canada. This is the least satisfactory method. In these cases the permanence of the cure depends on the period and quality of subsequent nursing. It is by this less desirable method that the Ukrainians of Canada were got united within a week of the writers first contact with them.

1. The Ukrainian Canadian Committee was formed in November 1940 after Professors George Simpson and Watson Kirkconnell, aided by Tracy Philipps, persuaded the Representative and Central Committees that existed within the Canadian Ukrainian population to coalesce. Precisely how this was accomplished is unclear.
2. Tracy Philipps arrived in Canada at the outbreak of World War Two. Describing himself as a "soldier on special service" he actively involved himself in Canadian Ukrainian affairs on behalf of Britain, arguing that since at least one-half of the war was going to be won in the mines, shipyards and factories of North America—where Ukrainians and other Slavs provided most of the heavy labour—the loyalty of these people had to be secured against fifth columnists of the Nazi-Soviet allegiance. He performed special tasks for the RCMP, worked with the Department of National War Services and played an influential, if not determinative, role in forcing the creation of a Ukrainian Canadian Committee in 1940. His activities remain largely unexplored.

actually worked in Ukraine had a lot to do with that. Apart from that, Tracy Philipps had what seemed to be a natural sympathy for Ukrainians, regardless of who they were. He had a tremendous effect on our policies and on our decisions in Canada. Both he and Dr. Kisilewsky (Kaye) played a very positive role in persuading Ukrainians in Canada to unite. While I never met Philipps in Canada before I left, I met him later overseas through correspondence, and often in person. He remained a supporter of our work until his death after World War Two.

Why did he play such a role in forming UCC? Well, I think that, by accident or by design, Tracy Philipps, as an available, yet retired, diplomat who knew Ukraine because he had served in post-World War One Ukraine with the Nansen International Office for Refugees, was used by the British to help bring in the Ukrainian Canadian population solidly behind the war effort. For a while Britain stood virtually alone in the war. They were very worried about fifth columns and subversion. And for them the only sure source of real material support was our Dominion. And in Canada, I think, they were convinced—and I'm glad they were—that the Ukrainian element was strong and would be supportive of their effort. In the first two years of the war we had given about 13 per cent of our Ukrainian Canadian population as voluntary recruits. So the governments—British and Canadian—were, I think at that time, convinced that they had to make a special effort to take an interest in the half million strong Ukrainian community in Canada, to make sure that it continued supporting the Allied war effort.

When he spoke to me and whenever he wrote to me, Philipps was always the man who promoted Dr. Kaye (Kisilewsky). He sponsored Kaye to England before the war because Kaye wanted to get a Ph.D. from an English university. Kaye was an historian, he wanted to do research. Kaye was also involved, I think seriously interested, in the Ukrainian liberation movement. I think Philipps helped him because Philipps was his "guardian." But it wasn't a coincidence that Kaye came to Canada and got a job in the Department of National War Services. He wasn't even Canadian, he was nothing in Canada. But he had a lot of security clearance and moral support from England, having the backing of people like Tracy Philipps, plus God knows who.

Philipps got involved and continued being involved even after the UCC was established. He went on a speaking tour during the war, trying to rally support for UCC and so on. He has a lot of support in the Ukrainian community in Canada in the beginning, and then the support faded. He was complaining bitterly about that, by 1943-44, that he was being ignored and not taken seriously. I think he became disenchanted with government circles too. Then he went back to Britain. He was very interested all the time in the Ukrainian cause. But I don't think there was anything more for him to do. I don't know what more he could have done. The only thing that would frustrate him, even more than I was frustrated, was the slow, unorthodox and somehow unrealistic approach of many of our people to getting things done. He was anxious to get things done at once. And the UCC in Winnipeg was slow and laborious—a peasant type of machine that never could make decisions or take action quickly it seemed, always narrow and short in its vision. You could never set Winnipeg on fire. At that time it frustrated him, and later it frustrated us very much when we formed CURB on our own initiative because of the urgency and magnitude of the refugee problem.

UCSA Establishes a Headquarters in London

Once established, I wrote to UCC and asked that we be admitted as a member organization. Now UCC was so young that it did not know how to deal with organizations who wanted to become members. UCC secretary was John Ruryk, a USRL man, ex-Cunard Line and CNR or CPR immigration and land settlement officer. When UCSA was organized we had dealings with John Ruryk first and later his successor, Tony Yaremovich, a young teacher from the Krydor, Saskatchewan district. Andrij Zaharychuk (from the UHO) became secretary after Mr. Yaremovich joined up. It took considerable "lobbying" in Winnipeg before UCC decided to support financially UCSA and its Services' Club. We were considered young, immature and likely not dependable or serious enough to run an organization and operate a club. After all, the average age of all the first members of UCSA was about twenty-four. Our own UCSA members came from every Ukrainian community in Canada. Many had no organizational background. Since we needed all the help we could get, we tried to keep all our Canadian Ukrainian organizations posted on what we were doing through our communiques to the Canadian Ukrainian press and our *UCSA Newsletter*. That helped generate enthusiasm back home for UCSA.

Once we decided to move UCSA to London, we had some trouble with the Manchester people because they had wanted us to keep our base there only and resented our move. They would have preferred Manchester to remain the central point of Ukrainian Canadian operations. We, on the other hand, felt that because so many Canadians were stationed close to London that we really should move the responsibilities of the Ukrainian Canadian operation to London. We did finally move in the summer of 1943. (The decision to open a UCSA Services Club in London was collectively made at our second Get-Together held in Manchester May 1943. The executive was also asked to call the next Get-Together in London, which was held July 31-August 1, 1943 at the Canadian Legion Services Club in Cartwright Gardens.) Since my service obligations took me to various parts of England and, after the invasion of Normandy, into France, Belgium, Holland and Germany, I visited London on weekends or my holidays only. We got the club organized by mail combined with the good will and voluntary work of those in the forces actually stationed in London or very near. Steve Kalin and I took lists of available properties from real estate agents and travelled from street to street looking for a permanent residence for UCSA. Eventually we found the Vicarage at 218 Sussex Gardens in Paddington. I called some members of the executive to London to see it, and we rented the building beginning in June 1943. I cabled UCC in Winnipeg: "Building for Services Club leased. Please cable $500 immediately for rent." John Ruryk claims to be the one who persuaded Dr. Kushnir and the UCC presidium to accept responsibility for rental of the Vicarage, but it wasn't easy. The UCC helped pay the rent. It was the best location we could find.

The military services weren't too happy with me at first. They checked up on me: what was I doing, where was I going. To do anything Ukrainian was considered politically suspect. I learned later that the Service Polish-Security often travelled to Manchester on the same trains I took—and back. In Digby I was twice called on the carpet by my superiors not for my organizational involvement in UCSA and the Social Club in Manchester,

54

but for "publishing names and locations of military units" in circular letters, which I inadvertently had done to help members visit one another. Canada was at war with Germany and here was a fellow organizing soldiers and airmen into an association based on a national or ethnic identity. Remember before the war in Canada there had been false rumours about the loyalty of the Ukrainians there. We proved these wrong by our enlistment, but some suspicions remained. So setting up a Ukrainian club was a bit tricky.

The Ukrainians of London

In London by 1941 (well after the fall of Czechoslovakia in 1939), there was an organization of Carpatho-Ukrainian refugees. How long it had existed I don't know for sure. But I have records of our contact with them. This group persisted until around 1947. The great thing that we got from these Ukrainians of Czech citizenship was a secretary for UCSA, Mrs. Maria Kowalska, who became secretary to our Central Ukrainian Relief Bureau (CURB) later on.

We found in London, incidentally, as we had in Manchester, an old Ukrainian community which became a pivot around which we operated, the remnants of the three other Ukrainian bureaux. Steve Davidovich, who had been director of the Ukrainian National Information Bureau in London, financed by nationalist organizations in North America and Europe, had volunteered for the Canadian armed forces and was employed as a clerk at Canadian Military Headquarters. He had married an English girl in London, and they had a home there, which they opened to Canadian servicemen. Of course, he became a member of our association. He was a corporal by then, a high rank at that time. So that was a bit of a nucleus. We also found Danylo Skoropadsky and his Hetman organization in London. He had a circle of English friends whom he brought to our club. For him it was a good front. It was good to be seen with Canadians while his father was living in Berlin. But I'm convinced that in his heart he was consciously and sincerely on our side. So we had him and his entourage, including Vladimir de Korostovetz, one-time Minister of External Affairs for Hetman Pavlo Skoropadsky. There was also the Ukrainian bureau that had been run by Dr. Kaye and financed by Mr. Mako-hon, another rather mysterious character.

I gather that Makohon had lived somewhere or other in Manitoba, near Winnipeg. Prior to the war around 1937 or 1938, he apparently married a very rich American. They opened a Ukrainian Information Office in Geneva and hired one of the World War One refugees, Evhen Bachinsky (ex-Ukrainian Red Cross) to run it. They opened another office in London and persuaded Dr. Kaye to look after that. He was in London then to do his Ph.D. In Geneva there was also another office run by Yaremijiv—a man who had been in the post-World War One Ukrainian National Republic's diplomatic corps. Both these gentlemen, Bachinsky and Yaremijiv, I met in Geneva after World War Two when I headed the Central Ukrainian Relief Bureau and did the Ukrainian Canadian Relief Fund's work in Europe. I used them as a nucleus around which to set up an affiliated Ukrainian Relief Committee in Switzerland, which operated from 1946-48.

The Nature of Our Club

Perhaps the strongest benefit of the UCSA was that it helped literally thousands of young men and women find or become more aware of their own Ukrainian identity. The key men and women in our organization, throughout the war and later in the relief mission, were people like myself who had come up through the ranks of the Ukrainian youth organizations in Canada. These organization people were, however, a minority. The number of young people from farms and towns who had joined the forces was much greater. Many of them could not speak or read Ukrainian, and many were not sure whether they were Orthodox or Catholic—thousands of them. But they gradually became aware and more consciously identified with being Ukrainian. They became part of the club, attended the alternating Orthodox/Catholic services, strengthening our fellowship there and maturing personally all the while. Literally hundreds began asking whether we had any literature about Ukraine and about Ukrainians in Canada. If you go through our files and archives and see the letters we wrote to UCC, we kept hammering away, "Send us literature. Send us books!" We established a library in London, a large library, which our servicemen were using extensively. All the Ukrainian publications were being received—*Svoboda* (Freedom), *Ukrainski Holos* (Ukrainian Voice), *Nouyi Shliakh* (New Pathway), *Ukrainski Visti* (Ukrainian News), *Kanadiiskyi Farmer* (Canadian Farmer), etc. Our reading-room was full of newspapers. You could find anything you wanted almost. And that had a tremendous effect on the servicemen (Canadian, American and even Polish and Czechoslovakian) that visited the club. They came and learned.

I think it is very often overlooked that about 75 per cent of these people were between eighteen and twenty-five years of age. They were all young, practically all single, only a few were middle aged. We had a number of weddings that took place at the London club, people meeting there for the first time and so on. I met my own wife, Anne Cherniawsky, there. We found that, as far as the members were concerned, it was only there that most of them began to find out about the history and geography of Ukraine, or Ukrainians in Canada. We would meet someone and ask them where they were from. "Innisfree, Alberta," they would say. "Where was that?" Nobody had ever heard of it before—or Meacham, or Hafford, or Krydor, Saskatchewan. Now those things *mean* something to all of us. But at that time we were all young people finding our common roots, together—the only thing we had otherwise to share was that we were in the Canadian armed forces, on the same side. Now the fact that somewhere back there we did have a common origin began to take up more of our attention. What roots there were was a rather vague matter for many before they discovered the club.

For those who came form the three Ukrainian Canadian youth associations, there was less to become aware of. But for those who came from the streets or farms, they were learning about their roots for the first time. They became some of our best workers once they were attracted and pitched in. For instance, in the London club we had absolutely no hired staff. We couldn't afford to hire anybody, but even if we could, there was no one available. The British were totally involved in the war. You couldn't find anyone to work in a private civilian job. The first more or less "permanent" caretaker we found was Thomas Zulak who managed to get himself released from the Polish forces. Later we got Teodor Turko the same way. But we did everything by ourselves! We drew up a schedule, we had a plan of operation. We had a duty club director, a duty secretary, a duty cleaner, etc., whatever you wanted. And whoever came to the club, whoever would be senior among them, would say to the others who came after him, "For the next two days this is your job." And everybody pitched in regardless of rank. I drew up a manual of standing orders and guidelines or instructions, from duty president to duty caretaker, much like an orderly officer or orderly non-commissioned officer in the service. Every job was written up to specifications with the maximum opportunity for personal initiative, and everyone had to write up his report after his tour of duty expired (which was generally twenty-four or forty-eight hours). It often happened that a private or corporal would be duty president or duty club director, while a captain—the rank automatically given to our dentists and doctors when they joined up—would be duty cook responsible for peeling potatoes. And next weekend positions and ranks could be reversed with the same or different personnel, all voluntary, based on honour and good will. It was a unique social setting.

Of course, one of the reasons they liked to come to the club was because they felt a kinship, a kindred spirit with others of Canadian Ukrainian background. But there was another reason, and I don't think it is something to be ashamed of: we didn't charge for anything. They slept at the club for nothing. They received cigarettes for nothing. They had coffee or snacks for nothing. The only contribution they had to make was to do some work. And because of this, I think people appreciated our service. We had a number of softball teams—tournaments in Hyde Park— we had a dance orchestra, a choir, and all of this was voluntary. It was a cheerful place to be, as even the *Winnipeg Free Press* called it, "A Homey Overseas Meeting Place" (19 April 1944).

And then there was this family. I don't know whether we found them, or they found us. Their name was Pankiw. They had been Canadians, living in Winnipeg in the 1930s, communists. Somewhere in 1937-38 just prior to the war, they decided to leave Canada and return to Ukraine—to the promised land, a Soviet paradise, that's what they expected—after having lived in Canada for many, many years. They had three girls, all born in Canada I think. They went to the Soviet Ukraine, thinking that since they were leftists and communists from Canada in this tremendously beautiful haven of newly established Soviet Ukraine, they would be gods, you see. Well, they found out very soon that they were prisoners. Their trunks were rifled. When they went to work somebody would invade the privacy of their home. Soviet security police, the NKVD, were always calling them in for interviews and so on. They were being treated as if they were Canadian and Western-planted spies or something. The regime made their lives so miserable there that the family got in touch with Wasyl Swystun, who was at that time still a patriotic Ukrainian, a lawyer in Winnipeg, and they begged him to get them out. He had settled their legal matters previously, for he was one of the early Ukrainian lawyers in Canada. They got in touch with him and said, "Help save us or we've had it." He was a good contact, a good lawyer, and since they were still Canadian citizens, they could be protected by Canada. So in 1939, just before the outbreak of the war, they managed to get to Riga, and from there they got on one of the last boats to London. By that time the war was on full blast, and they could not get any further than London. So they stayed there, waiting for the war to end and hoping to get back to Canada. We found them and established contact.

They were so happy to see us they threw their home open to us—another home away from home. We were Canadians and they had been, only now they had been enlightened by personal Soviet experience. They were lonely for Canada. Mr. Pankiw was working somewhere in some National Service job as area warden or something. He was also a very good carpenter, I believe. Mrs. Pankiw and the girls were regular visitors to the club and helped us tremendously. Mrs. Pankiw was a mother to all of us. One of the girls joined the Auxiliary Territorial Service (ATS). Every Sunday we would always have a formal dinner where they would be the chief cooks and bottle-washers. With our own girls, service people and so on, they worked like beavers. For they were people who could provide continuity. When the war ended they went back to Canada, to Vancouver. But at that time they were a tremendous help to us.

The others helping out at the club were all local service personnel. Anne Cherniawsky was employed by RCAF headquarters in London in the Pay Accounts Department. That was a permanent job for her, and she was living in private billets. Emily Winarski was another girl employed there. When we eventually found them, through contacts in Canada who wrote to them urging them to visit the club, we persuaded them to give up their private quarters and move into the club. They didn't have to pay anything at our place. They had a private room that they shared. But the condition was that they would help in looking after the place during their off-duty time. So in a very short while, Anne Cherniawsky became director of the club and Emily Winarski became an assistant secretary. Their presence plus our luck in getting the Pawsey family (an English family) to move in and live in the basement flat as caretakers assured the survival of the club. At Canadian Military Headquarters, there was Ann Crapleve, who came to us as a corporal, but who was soon commissioned a lieutenant in administration and was a tremendous asset in operating the club. She became our treasurer. Soon we had ten to fifteen officers who were regularly helping around the club. That also helped our status.

Chaplains for UCSA

One of the initial things we did when UCSA was first organized in 1943 was to petition the military authorities for our own chaplains from the Ukrainian Catholic (Uniate) and Ukrainian Orthodox faiths. In this matter we sent special memoranda to Canada House, to Canadian Military Headquarters, to RCAF headquarters and to the Department of National War Services in Ottawa. Ottawa heeded our pleas, especially since they were supported by UCC, both Ukrainian churches and all the Ukrainian organizations at home. You see, when war broke out and heavy recruiting and mobilization started there were only two recognized religious categories for all Canadians—either you were Protestant (P), or you were Roman Catholic (RC). We Ukrainians were neither. But Canadian history had not yet discovered that Canada was more than English (P) and French (RC). So every recruit was asked, "Are you Catholic?" If he said yes, he was labelled "RC," if he said no, he was tabbed "P." So Ukrainian Catholics and Ukrainian Orthodox believers, Jews, Muslims, what have you, were left out, or inaccurately labelled. It is different now. We are much wiser.

So Ukrainian priests came over in the summer of 1944— Father Semen Sawchuk (Ukrainian Orthodox) and Father Michael Horoshko (Ukrainian Catholic) as military chaplains with the rank of Honorary Captain. That helped. They visited the military units stationed in the United Kingdom and persuaded Ukrainian service personnel to come and visit our club. At the end of the war when we had our last Get-Together in London, November 10-11, 1945, we must have had close to a thousand servicemen parade up and down London. We couldn't have a church service in our club because it was much too small. So all the Ukrainian Catholics went off to a Roman Catholic church (St. Edward's Convent) while we Orthodox went to St. James' next door.

The Emerging Problem of Ukrainian Displaced Persons and Refugees

Many of us who were deeply involved in the club were also committed to active military operations in Europe. I happened to be one of those who was with the Second Tactical Air Force and went to Normandy with the 126th wing of the RCAF in 1944. I went with the advance D-Day military invasion forces and was one of the first two Canadian air force officers to land in Normandy. Our Second Tactical Air Force had fighter squadrons—Spitfires—three squadrons per wing. Our job was to support the invading troops, Montgomery's Second Army, of which the Canadian Corps was a part. You couldn't find a Canadian fighting unit in which there weren't some Ukrainians. In fact, by that time, the legend in Europe among the Ukrainian Displaced Persons (DPS) was that marching alongside the Canadian forces there was a Ukrainian army coming to "liberate" them.

We, on the other hand, had heard by that time of the Ukrainian Division "Galicia" through Allied intelligence.[1] One of the first dead youths I found in Normandy was a young Ukrainian lad in German uniform—I still have the documents somewhere. The Germans used Ukrainians as slave workers and young teenagers

---

1. For additional material on the Ukrainian Division "Galicia," see Roger James Bender and Hugh Page Taylor, *Uniforms, Organization and History of the Waffen-SS* 4 (San Jose, 1975); Wasyl Veryha, *Dorohamy Druhoyi Svitovoyi Viyny* (Toronto: New Pathway Publishers, 1980); or General Pavlo Shandruk, *Arms of Valor* (New York, 1959).

were forced to man anti-aircraft units in defence of the "Atlantic Wall." To build their fortifications, the Nazis also exploited slave labour which they mobilized into their Todt Organization. These were Ukrainians from central or East Ukraine. Since most German males were in the *Wehrmacht,* or if unfit for military service at home running the farms, they imported millions of these foreign labourers. Ukrainians from Poland were made to wear "P" badges. From Soviet Ukraine the labourers wore an "Ost" badge. They were the *Ost-arbeiters* (East Workers). Western Europe was full of these people. That is how I first got in contact with Ukrainian refugees and began to realize the dimensions of the refugee problem. Canadian Ukrainians were still largely unaware of what was coming or happening in Europe. All our links to Ukrainians there had been cut off by the war.

From that time on I was on active duty in Europe up until the middle of 1946, except for my leaves. But I kept running the club by remote control, through correspondence, writing circular letters to the executive and the membership. I would write letters, instructions, issue directives. They went to the people who were in London, the club director and any executive or committee members left in the England. At that time the UCSA vice presidents for the United Kingdom were Capt. Peter Smylski and Capt. Michael Lucyk (both dentists). They got to England towards the end of the war and were stationed in the south. Michael Lucyk took the job of editing our *UCSA Newsletter*. Peter acted as my deputy and would make decisions for me; they worked as a team, looking after the details. All I did was issue directives in the form of Executive Circulars. They sent me regular reports and every holiday or leave I had, I went to London.

By that time, once the Allies had breached Hitler's "Fortress Europe," UCSA members began thinking about having Get-Togethers not only in London, but elsewhere. For example, Bill Kereliuk and the boys in the Mediterranean Theatre organized a social Get-Together in Rome for Christmas 1945, which Bishop Ivan Buchko helped sponsor and attended. They even set up a UCSA Services nucleus there. We also had a Get-Together in Paris, and two in Brussels. Father Maxim Hermaniuk (now Metropolitan) celebrated mass for our first Brussels Get-Together. He was then just an ordinary Redemptorist Catholic priest and a refugee in Belgium. For the first Get-Together we organized in Brussels November 25-26, 1945, three priests celebrated Mass for the Ukrainians in the liberation forces and their own community, of course. Our servicemen did the "chanting." Mykola Hrab was president of the Ukrainian community organization in Belgium. He had been living there since before the war. Around his people we eventually built up a Ukrainian Relief Committee in Belgium, which also allied itself later with CURB. We also opened a UCSA Services Club in Brussels.

The further Allied forces advanced into Holland and Germany, the more our own efforts grew. We did the same thing wherever we went. Wherever we found Ukrainians, we got them together and organized committees. We told them, "Come on, we'll help you but you've got to stand on your own two feet." Before we came they had no organized relief committees amongst themselves. Nothing. Every relief committee that was organized on the Continent was organized by us, directly or indirectly. We would mail out instructions, or physically bring people together whenever we could. In Holland it went slowly. Most Ukrainians there drifted into Belgium where there were established (now revived) organizations. Eventually Ukrainian organizations did get started in Holland. In Germany Ukrainian organizations were set up in each occupation zone. In Austria it was the same. The zones were established as soon as the Allies came in and these territories were liberated. Of course, Allied service personnel had no access to the Soviet Zone, but as far as the other three went (French, British and American), we did. So we immediately established contacts with whatever Ukrainian refugees we could find. By that time they were looking for us, so contact was easy. In France there were two Ukrainian committees: one headed by Father Perridon, the other by Father Brenzan, the Orthodox priest. Eventually we married the two committees together under Father Perridon.

Everywhere I was stationed I was getting visitors and delegations practically on a daily basis. The news had spread through the refugee and displaced persons' grapevine. Nobody could control these DP movements, there was always a certain amount of chaos. So I was getting delegations in Germany, already, from the Ukrainian government-in-exile. I had a delegation from Bishop

Ivan Buchko, who was in Rome and morally felt that the Roman Catholic church was responsible for Ukrainian Catholics now in the DP camps in western Europe. I also met a delegation in Munich who came from Metropolitan Polikarp, head of the Synod of Bishops of the Orthodox church. They were bringing me letters and reports about the state of the refugee situation where they were located, and I was sending all this information back to UCC in Winnipeg and to the United Ukrainian American Relief Committee (UUARC) in Philadelphia, all through military channels. The forces of occupation were the only channel of communication for almost a year. The mail service in Germany was disrupted, and they couldn't send letters to Canada or the United States. We (the Ukrainian Canadians in the occupation forces) were the only means of communication in 1945-46. That perhaps was our greatest immediate emergency contribution as western territories were liberated, that and saving refugees from forcible repatriation.

Rev. Kushnir Visits Europe

I was stationed at Utersen near Hamburg when Rev. Dr. Kushnir, the president of UCC, came overseas on his fact-finding tour of Europe. He was present at our eleventh UCSA Get-Together, Ukrainian Christmas 1946, and at my wedding, February 2, 1946. He really came to supervise the closing of our club. It took us over a month to get permission for him to visit some DP camps in Germany. I took him on the first lap of the journey through the British Zone.

Kushnir's greatest contribution to our work and efforts was his positive support, as president of UCC, which resulted in financial assistance first for UCSA, then for the Central Ukrainian Relief Bureau. I was convinced of that right from the first day I met him on his arrival in England. We had had correspondence, and so on, but I never knew him before. But I knew of him when I was still teaching in Yellow Creek. I knew of him when negotiations for forming UCC started in 1938. He represented the whole Catholic movement. And he was the president of BUC at that time. And he was sort of an irreplaceable president of BUC. Nobody else in that organization seemed to be very interested in what was happening to the Ukrainians, except Kushnir. In some of our own USRL files, our organizational reports and so on, over and over and over again comes this business of Kushnir being a wheeler and dealer. Kossar, of course, was just the same, only in UNF, but these were one-man shows. And Kushnir was, perhaps, a force within BUC.

When Kushnir came to England, he took special time off from UCC and his church. He didn't really do anything concrete all the time he was there, except he put on a good front. He was a good representative. His greatest contribution was that we had a president of UCC. We could say, "This is the president of UCC, he represents the *whole* Ukrainian Canadian community." And the president of UCC does that. But he couldn't talk to all people. First of all, his English was poor, he could hardly speak English. We had to pave the way for him, and I took him around. Once he was amongst Ukrainians, then, of course, he was at home. We couldn't really do things on our own. We had to knock on doors, we weren't even a strong lobby. But we needed a lobby and people like Kushnir couldn't lobby. We could do a certain amount if we had the right person at the right place at the right time. When the first DPs met Kushnir, many of them honestly believed that we had the potential of raising an army, that I was a commander—even if it was a secret commander—that there was an army of Ukrainians coming from Canada to save, that is liberate, Ukraine. It was a legend for a while. They felt just because a person had a uniform—I was an RCAF intelligence officer, and my job was to brief pilots, to tell them where to go, what their targets were, and when they came back to interview them and report to higher command on whether the mission was carried out or not. That's all. They thought I was in espionage, and God knows what and where. So the same fiction, I think, grew up around Kushnir. It would be interesting to know what happened to Kushnir's archives and files, if anything.

Solely through us at the beginning, UCC was made aware of what was going on.[1] I'm sure that many must have foreseen there would be a refugee problem, but nobody appreciated the magnitude of it—not thousands or tens or hundreds of thousands of people, but millions of refugees. What could UCC do? The only

---

1. The first Ukrainian Canadian Committee Congress was held in Winnipeg, between June 22-24, 1943. In the published proceedings of this national meeting, there is only one minor reference to the problem of Ukrainian DPs.

65

thing was write to us and say, "Look up somebody," or "Give us more information on this or that," or "What do you think about that?" To me many of those problems at that time were new problems. There were new names to learn, the history of the political and social movements in Ukraine to learn about—luckily I learned quickly. But there was little about this then that UCC or the American Ukrainians could do immediately.

The displaced persons were of various kinds and categories: "P" workers, *Ost-arbeiters,* voluntary workers, families of workers, or Ukrainians in German uniforms, slave workers in the Todt engineering organization, the political refugees of OUN and genuine refugees fleeing the Red Army returning to Ukraine. We found them, in many cases in groups or clusters, already living in large German establishments that were left vacant at the end of the war—factories, warehouses, military barracks and the like. These later became the nuclei of the DP camps which were merged together or moved as became necessary. At the very beginning in Germany, that is in June 1945, I found near Hamburg, for instance, about fifty Ukrainian girls in a munitions factory. They asked, "What do we do?" All I could say was, "Just stay here. Somehow somebody is going to take care of you."

Encounters with DPs

At first few people were concerned about these DPs—they were nobody's responsibility, not even the Germans! As soon as the Allied military government was set up, it had to look after them. There were also thousands of people who were on the move at the end of the war, fleeing ahead or alongside the Germans, retreating westward from the Soviet East—refugees. Germany and Austria were filled with such unfortunates. They were people who were running away, escaping from the advancing Soviet armies, salvaging what they could. In many cases they had no papers or documents of any kind at all. They would just settle down in a group, and the military government would have to do something about them. Otherwise they'd block the roads, clog transport systems and impede our troops' freedom of movement. There were already a lot of refugees before the war ended, people our armies freed as they moved deeper into the Third Reich. With those refugees, in particular, one of the big problems was establishing who they were. Many of them had no documents; they had lost them, or destroyed them on purpose. Those who were in Germany and who had been there for a year or two had something. But those who had just come in had nothing.

There were links between the small community of emigré Ukrainians from post-World War One days in Geneva—Yaremijiv, Bachinsky—plus some new refugees like Metropolitan Ilarion, Warsaw MP Milena Rudnitska—and the Ukrainian community in Paris. Bachinsky had worked in the 1920s with the Ukrainian Red Cross. In that capacity, he had been associated with the International Red Cross in Geneva. Milena Rudnitska, a former member of the Polish *Sejm* (Parliament), managed to get into Switzerland very quickly, perhaps even before hostilities ceased. They were aware of the fact that establishing identities would be one of the major postwar problems. So they printed Ukrainian Red Cross identity cards. They sent a few emissaries into Germany and Austria with loads of these cards to issue to people who needed one. One of the people came to me because by that time everybody knew that Panchuk "a Canadian officer" was there, and there were still legends about our Canadian Ukrainian effort circulating—that I had "thousands of people" under my "command" and so on. They brought me a stack of these cards, so we issued them.

We organized meetings in forests, bushes and camps. I had a portable typewriter and a military jeep, and people like F/L Jerry Burianyk, an engineering officer in my unit, would come with me. And these refugees would line up and we issued these Red Cross cards to them. I'd sign my own name as authorization. We must have issued three, four, or maybe five thousand of those spurious Ukrainian Red Cross cards until the authorities caught up with the fact that these cards were not really legitimate. Later on the British military authorities arrested some of the fellows who were distributing these identity documents. Dr. Homzin was one of them. We had to bail them out. I had to go to the British authorities and explain that in such a crisis, an emergency, there was a need for some sort of personal identity document. It was a question of saving lives. Generally speaking, the British authorities were very understanding and receptive to these things.

DP Camps in Europe, 1945

Legend:
- – – – 1937 boundaries
- – – Occupation zones
- ■ Central headquarters
- ⊙ Zone headquarters
- · Refugee camps

Baltic Sea

North Sea

Kiel

Bremerhaven

Hamburg

Bremen

Weser

Elbe

U.S.S.R.

Berlin

Wunstorf

B R I T I S H   Z O N E

Lemgo

Bielefeld

ZONE

Halle

Düsseldorf

Arolsen

Weimar

Cologne

Bonn

Coblence

Rhine

Frankfurt

U N I T E D   S T A T E S

Wiesbaden

F R E N C H

Z O N E

Regensburg

Danube

Stuttgart

Z O N E

Tübingen

Haslach

Pasing

Munich

Freiburg

N

0   50   100
KILOMETRES

Saving lives, yes. You have to understand how much that meant. Just after the war there was a "big hunt" on by the Soviets at about the same time as the United Nations Relief and Rehabilitation Administration (UNRRA) was initiating its operations. The UNRRA was the result of international deliberations like the Atlantic Conference, San Francisco Conference and, above all, the Yalta Agreement of February 1945, between Churchill, Roosevelt and Stalin. One of the most important Soviet aims, of which the West was, on the whole, ignorant, was to get as many of these Ukrainian, Russian, Baltic and other eastern European refugees back to their side of the Iron Curtain as quickly as possible. And that was done on the basis of the Yalta Agreement: each Allied country would repatriate its own nationals immediately after they were liberated and hostilities ceased, and each would help the other in this matter. Few servicemen in the West were even aware of the Yalta Agreement and what it was really all about. But the Soviets knew. And they insisted that the West send these "Soviet citizens" back. Repatriating people to their areas of origin became one of the postwar problems—then called relief and rehabilitation. The Soviets had helped set up the UNRRA and were on its executive councils, so they had great influence.

UNRRA was committed to assist in the repatriation of Soviet citizens, and anyone they decreed to be a Soviet citizen was supposed to go back. We thought, at first, when we learned about it that this was a voluntary thing. But the Soviets demanded that it be compulsory, that people *had* to go back regardless of their wishes. In fact, in many places where they (the Soviet repatriation officers) were free to roam, they would stop a civilian in the street, and if they found a Ukrainian, they would very often load him into a jeep or vehicle and that was it. I was reading in my diary about an incident in 1945 when four Soviet officers came and picked up the leader of a Ukrainian group, Olya. Next time I came to visit the group, she was gone. A Soviet jeep had called on them with a Ukrainian-speaking Red Army lieutenant. They had taken her to the Soviet "Welcome Home" Repatriation Camp nearby—Folingbostle. We tried to rescue her. The trail took us to the camp, but stopped there. We were refused entry and they claimed to have no information about Olya. She just disappeared.

People were forcibly repatriated. No doubt about it. We tried to follow it up, F/L Stewart and I, but there was regular daily train transport operating from the repatriation camp straight across the Soviet border. Olya was gone. Thousands of others went the same way before anybody realized what was happening. Forcible repatriation became quite an issue in 1945-46. I was stationed near Hamburg at the time. Major Michael Syrotiuk (from Edmonton), a Canadian Ukrainian officer in the military government, was near Copenhagen. I got a telegram from him, "Do something immediately! 365 Ukrainians are going to be shipped off to the Soviet Union tomorrow." What could I do except send a telegram to Winnipeg and the same to Philadelphia. And they, in turn, sent telegrams of protest to Ottawa and Washington. Sometimes these helped block such shipments, sometimes not. We did what we could. Still hundreds and thousands were sent back against their will.

How many actually were forced and how many went back willingly, it is hard to say. There are no statistics on that. I have a sneaking suspicion that more went back to Ukraine voluntarily than were forced, but that's only a suspicion. For many of the ordinary working peasants, who were in Germany or Austria as slave labourers, I think that the Soviet propaganda was strong enough to say "Come home," and they would go back. Homesickness, their bad experiences in the West under German rule, the uncertainty of the refugee period—all that would militate in favour of people going back—and some were just naive. UNRRA and later on the International Relief Organization (IRO) objected very much to the activities of those Ukrainians who were a little bit more intelligent, like Ivan Bahrianyi, who was conscious of the communist situation in East Ukraine and agitated against the DPs return there.[1] Such activists did go around to the DP camps and try to explain to people that, "Look, you're going back out of the frying pan into the fire." And the Soviets, of course, picked that up and that's what created difficulties for Canadian Ukrainian

---

1. Ivan Bahrianyi, *Why I Do Not Want To Go "Home"* (1947) (first published in *The Ukrainian Quarterly* II, no. 3 (1946)) was highly influential in explaining to the Allies why many Ukrainians refused to return to the USSR. Bahrianyi was an East Ukrainian publicist and founding member of the Ukrainian Revolutionary Democratic Party.

refugee relief efforts. UNRRA and IRO said, "We allow these Canadian Ukrainians to visit DP camps." The Soviets countered, "How do we know that these 'representatives' aren't coming to start 'agitating' against repatriation?" We insisted that the DPs should get Ukrainian newspapers from Canada, that they should be allowed to distribute these. But the occupation authorities worried—what news did these papers contain? What outlook did they promote? Were they anti-Soviet, anti-repatriation, inflammatory? So for some time they banned newspapers from Canada and the United States because of their "agitation." Communists and fellow travellers often working as "officers" in UNRRA were largely responsible for this. A lot of the people had good intentions, but our involvement complicated things for them—agitation on both sides, for staying and for returning.

I would imagine not only that the naive, poor, peasant, East Ukrainian, who was homesick and wanted to go back to his village, but also large numbers, who were not acclimatized to the West, also went back to Ukraine. Apart from these who went voluntarily for legitimate, emotional reasons, I wouldn't be surprised that some went back to see if they couldn't take the opportunity to get back into the countryside and get in touch with the underground (Ukrainian Insurgent Army—UPA) still there. The OUN and Supreme Ukrainian Liberation Council (UHVR) had their couriers between western Europe and Ukraine until the late 1940s, if not beyond. There remained a limited and difficult circulation between the refugees and the homeland, but it did exist.

The UCC could not do much by itself. The Canadian government was still too afraid of any Canadian Ukrainian activities that had any political tinge to them. UCC had a political—anti-Soviet—colouration. So it was suggested, and the federal government accepted this, that a separate relief body or organization be set up to help the Ukrainian DPs. The same people who were executive officers of the UCC became executive officers in the Ukrainian Canadian Relief Fund, a totally separate purely relief organization theoretically. For a while it was registered with the Canadian Red Cross and affiliated with it. In fact, in their first few months, or maybe year of operation, their letterhead said "Ukrainian Canadian Relief Fund (UCRF), affiliated with the Canadian Red Cross." That's formally how our efforts were organized. But the UCRF headquarters was in Winnipeg while the DP problems were in Europe, especially in Germany, Austria and Italy. People had to be there to be effective helpers. Eventually the Canadian Red Cross people got too embarrassed to keep up the link with UCRF—it had too political a quality. So it then took on an independent existence. Nevertheless, the Canadian Red Cross formally made us Red Cross members and representatives in 1946 for operations in Europe.

The United Ukrainian American Relief Committee

In the United States at almost the same time as UCC was established in Canada, the Ukrainian American Congress Committee was being formed. The two committees kept communicating with each other. The first Congress in Canada was held in Winnipeg in June 1943. UCSA was already in existence, active, and had held two large Get-Togethers in Manchester. We even sent greetings to the Congress. Aid for the UCSA (Active Service Overseas) Services Club in London was a major item in UCC plans during the war years. In the United States it was also foreseen that some relief to refugees in Europe would be needed. The American Ukrainians, we found, seemed to be able to foresee the acute need for aid and welfare for Ukrainian war victims and DPs, but neither Ukrainians in the United States, nor our own people in Canada could really appreciate the urgency and the magnitude of the DP problem in the immediate postwar years.

In the United States there was a Ukrainian relief committee formed in Philadelphia and another in Detroit. I am not sure which came first. One of the key men in Philadelphia was Dr. Walter Gallan, a World War One Ukrainian veteran and immigrant. One of the key men in Detroit was a lawyer, John Panchuk, Canadian-born (but no relation). Later these two committees united to form the United Ukrainian American Relief Committee. John Panchuk became the president and Walter Gallan the executive director.

Various Ukrainian-language newspapers arrived at the London club from both Canada and the United States, so we were able to follow these North American events. Whenever problems arose overseas, now at least, we had addresses from the newspapers to write back home to—these were our first contacts. We based all our hopes on subsequent cooperation from both Philadelphia and Winnipeg. They, in turn, authorized me personally to become their on-the-spot relief mission. Eventually our initiative helped form relief committees in Turkey, Norway, Sweden, Argentina, Brazil, Paraguay, Uruguay, Peru and almost every country in western Europe.

How Best to Help?

All of this work for the Ukrainian DPs didn't go unnoticed. Some of my colleagues in the Canadian forces were perturbed because I was so involved in refugee affairs by 1945-46. Even Father Michael Horoshko was also getting worried. Therefore, while I was on the Continent, a special UCSA meeting was called in London, in February 1945, in my absence at which I was criticized for my actions and activities—they were considered to be too political and might bring sanctions upon UCSA from the Allied military authorities. I couldn't accept that. I believed it was our moral duty and obligation to try to help these Ukrainian victims of war to the maximum of our abilities. We were doing humanitarian work—we were still serving as Canadian servicemen—who could deny us our relief work? But others disagreed. So I sent in my resignation as UCSA president. Father M. Horoshko, I believe, was the leader of this revolt. When my resignation was received the UCSA executive still in London called another meeting and formally turned down my resignation and gave me a total and unanimous vote of confidence. F/L William Kereliuk was then acting secretary and it was he who helped re-establish stability in UCSA at this time.

UCSA Transformed: the Central Ukrainian Relief Bureau

Still, just as the period of transition from UCSA to CURB activities was taking place, it was touch-and-go whether we would "stick together"; when there was a fear that we were getting over-involved and that it all might get very embarrassing, especially because there were moments when, perhaps under a different regime, I might have been court-martialled—for affairs, like that of the Ukrainian Red Cross identity cards incident—several Canadian Ukrainians backed away from refugee relief work. Perhaps they should not be overly faulted. We all had military duties to perform, yet here we were interferring with people who were being

73

arrested and put into the klink—like Doroshenko in Brussels, Dmytro Donsow in London and others, some of whom were accused of being war collaborators and criminals. As soon as the Germans were out of Belgium, it was a common thing for one Belgian to point a finger at another and claim, "She's a collaborator. Yesterday she was sleeping with a German." It was easy for any foreigner in Belgium and France to get into trouble. He had to keep his mouth shut and stay inside. Foreigners were very easily suspect. Ukrainian DPs had to be careful. Let me give you an example.

Mykola Hrab came to me one day in Brussels and said, "Look you've got to help. About fifteen Ukrainians were arrested, picked up off the street yesterday by the Belgians and interned in that school building." They were there in a gymnasium, sleeping on straw. God knows what for. I couldn't even speak French, but Hrab could. And I just said to the authorities, "I'm a Canadian officer and these are Ukrainians and I've spoken with them and know who they are. I'll take responsibility for them." And they were released. I had no business doing that! No right at all. That was how we commonly had to operate. People were coming to me all the time with such requests. I'd be in the officers' mess and a phone call would come in from the guard at the main gate, "Flight Lieutenant Panchuk, there's someone here at the gate to see you." I'd go out and there's a delegation with requests that had nothing to do with our military operations in Germany. But we'd have to do something. We cared, and so we worked.

Getting in Touch with Our Ukrainian Division "Galicia"

Up until that time, few Canadian Ukrainians knew of the Ukrainian Division "Galicia." Delegations came to see us with information about this military formation. I had some access to literature so we knew they had laid down their arms before the British in Austria and had been sent, route march, across the Alps to camps near Rimini, Italy. Refugees who were in Germany had brought me information and news about them, which I sent on to UCC in Winnipeg and UUARC in Philadelphia. Some we translated into English for the British and American authorities. We did all we could to familiarize the West with the background of the Division, who they were, where they were and so on. We wanted to make certain that they were not unjustly treated as war criminals of Nazis, since we knew quite a bit about them.

There was one very interesting incident relating to them when they were already in Rimini. We were in London in 1946. Flight Lieutenant Joseph Romanow, an RCAF pilot and an excellent UCSA officer, had been posted back to England after flying in the China-India-Burma Theatre. He was there preparatory to returning to Canada for discharge. While in England he was flying service trips to Paris, Brussels, Frankfurt—the main European cities—carrying VIPs. His job was to pilot a DC3-Dakota. One day he came to the club and said, "Look, I'm going to Rome tomorrow. Anybody want to come along?" I said, "Well, I can't go, I'm tied up and returning to Germany." But Capt. Peter Smylski, who had a whole week off, said, "I'll go, but how do we do it?" Well Joe said, "I know the route blindfolded. I fly it all the time. So I don't need an Observer Navigator. My navigator is going to appreciate having a few extra days of holiday here in London, so his uniform is available." So Peter Smylski, a dentist, became an RCAF uniformed officer with an Observer's badge and Flight Lieutenant in rank. He sat in the navigator's seat beside Joe Romanow and off they went to Rome.

Our purpose was to take advantage of this rare opportunity to establish direct contact with the Ukrainian Catholic Bishop Ivan Buchko, who chaired the Ukrainian Relief Committee in Rome, and through him with the Division, who, as I have said, were being held in Rimini as SEP (Surrendered Enemy Personnel). We had already received certain mail from Canada and the United States that we wanted to pass on to these people, which we couldn't do directly. And we knew from Bishop Buchko that there was mail there that had to go to Canada and the United States. The other purpose was a desire for first-hand information and contact. So Romanow and Smylski met with Bishop Buchko. He had to send his emissaries to Rimini to get the material we wanted, and Joe Romanow had to stall his return to England by claiming inclement weather en route. The next day, even though the weather was beautiful in Rome, Romanow told the waiting VIPs, "Look, the weather is pretty bad. I guess we'd better stay a day or two longer." So they stayed three days in Rome in order to complete their mission. The people they took down there had to stay longer than they expected, but our team had performed its mission. We got direct links set up with Rimini. That was how we eventually helped move them to England during mid to late 1947. By late 1948 most were civilianized there.

Later we received much more information about the Division through messages and contacts in Germany—people like Professor Kubijovych, who had been one of those who had helped set up this formation in Lviv during the war. He could give us all the relevant details. Anything more we needed we could get because between the DPs in Germany and the Rimini group there was an underground courier system circulating information all the time. The British authorities in London didn't really know what we were doing. Those at the military bases where we were stationed didn't mind. Most military men were very friendly to the Ukrainians. At Rimini there were two officers, a British colonel and a captain, who were in charge of our Ukrainian SEPs. They were very friendly men, they liked their charges. These British officers heard directly from the Division's men why the Division was formed and who it fought. They knew that in the Canadian armed forces there were thousands and thousands of Ukrainians. We were loyal Canadians and we were helping those in Rimini, so, they reasoned, their prisoners must be decent men. You know our strong position with the British and Canadian authorities, and later on with the Americans, rested on this fact—that we had such a large number of active servicemen, Canadian Ukrainians who had voluntarily supported the Allied war effort. The Allied authorities exchanged communications. We were always in touch with Canada House. Everyone knew that Canadian Ukrainians had fully earned a say in Western affairs by dint of their sacrifices. So that, shortly after the war's end, when we had all this information and I was still in uniform, the War Office in London called me in and made me a firm offer. "Look, we'd like you to be our advisor, our consultant on Ukrainian affairs."

I agreed. And they in turn agreed not to do anything on Ukrainian matters, especially the Ukrainian Division "Galicia," without my advice. "You're in touch with the Ukrainian community in Canada and the authorities there. The Canadian authorities in Ottawa will listen more to the Ukrainian Canadians who are there and who have their people at home growing Canada's

wheat, than to Canada House or to us here. So it's up to you.''
And a lot of the information about Ukrainian DPS was channelled
through me back to Canada and to British and American officials.
When the question arose of moving the Division from Rimini to
the United Kingdom between May and October 1947, I was con-
sulted on it. I went down to Italy and helped close up the camp. I
even made a film of the closing of the camp. I put the Ukrainians
aboard a train with British officers en route to the ships. The latter
then turned over to me all the money they had taken from censor-
ing the letters received by the internees from the United States and
Canada—thousands of dollars—I put it in my car and smuggled
it across the Alps to England. When they arrived in England I met
them in Sheffield, greeting them as they disembarked. I organized
them into various committees for the different camps and hostels
where they were being sent to around Britain. The British War
Office permitted me to take some of these soldiers to London to
work at CURB, which was formed by now—they couldn't sleep in
town since technically they were all now prisoners of war, so they
were posted to a former POW camp for Germans located near London and given bus passes to commute to our offices. These men
were very helpful to me—they distributed money back to the
rightful owners, compiled statistics on who was where, visited
camps to see what welfare help was needed and generally kept us
fully informed on the affairs of these relocated soldiers now that
they were in Britain.

The Association of Ukrainians in Great Britain Develops

CURB also engaged people like Steve Yaworsky, formerly of the
Polish air force. On January 19, 1946 we had helped establish a
fairly strong and viable Association of Ukrainians in Great Britain
(AUGB). Initially there had been formed an Association of Ukrainian Soldiers in the Polish Armed Forces—it consisted almost
entirely of Ukrainians serving in the Polish forces under British
command during the war and the civilians who had come with
them to Britain. We literally compelled these Ukrainians, and
there were hundreds of them, to get organized. And we gave them
the use of UCSA facilities at 218 Sussex Gardens. They could come
there, live there, just as our own UCSA members had done. They
had keys to the place. They set up their own press and newspaper,

Nasha Meta (Our Aim). But that was only for the Ukrainians in the Polish forces. As soon as we had the Division's men in England in 1947, we could not fit in or cope with European Voluntary Workers and others arriving from the DP camps as well in just a servicemen's organization. So we put on a larger hat. We reorganized and changed the name to AUGB, to which everyone could belong. We knew that our time in England was limited, that it would eventually be up to them once the Canadian Ukrainians went back home. So we got all of the Ukrainians arriving in England to organize and stand up on their own strength and resources. We were helping create in England the infrastructure for an organized British Ukrainian life—something that had been all but nonexistent before the war.

I was only a shadow president at first. The AUGB's first president was Mr. Mykyta Bura, now living in Toronto. He was an ex-member of the Polish *Sejm,* not a soldier, but a diplomat, a solid character with time on his hands. His sons were in the Polish forces, actually with the RAF Polish wing. George Jenkala, a Ukrainian soldier in the Polish army, became the AUGB secretary. Others who were in England at this time were F/O M. Oparenko, F/O G. Salsky and F/L S. Nahnyhda—all three Polish air force officers, serving with the RAF, came to work for AUGB.

Now that the war was over, the problem of political involvement by service personnel didn't exist to the same degree. Most of the UCSA executive, voluntary workers and all of my friends were back in Canada. There were only some latecomers to England left in London, who had little priority for repatriation, and we started leaning on them very heavily—Bill Byblow, Mike Krysowaty and others. I applied to the RCAF headquarters for an extension of my service overseas. This was granted and I was posted once again to Germany to serve another year with the occupation forces.

We had a meeting of all people left at 218 Sussex Gardens— among them Capt. Smylski, F/L Romanov, Capt. Father Horoshko—and I said, "Okay, if working for our Ukrainian refugees is a delicate thing, how do we go about it? Couldn't we form a separate relief bureau?" It was the only answer. So we just there and then called into being the Central Ukrainian Relief Bureau (CURB). That's all. There was no justification. There was no

78

authority. There was no request. Nobody yet knew anything about it. We just got together there, talked, then said, "As of now we are CURB. Its operational records begin on September 15, 1945, although, formally, we only started on December 31, 1945. For a while UCSA and CURB existed side by side as parallel but separate organizations, and I headed both.

We were going to bombard UCC in Winnipeg hard, confront UUARC in Philadelphia and tell all our Ukrainians in North America that we had created CURB and that they *must* be our sponsors. Our resources were too limited. I had been appointed by UCC to be director of CURB and to be responsible for all relief work on behalf of both the Ukrainian Canadian Relief Fund and the United Ukrainian American Relief Committee Limited, but I was still on active service overseas. We were trying to meet the Ukrainian refugees' urgent needs. My general instructions from UCC in Winnipeg when they appointed me were, "Do whatever you think must be done." Quite a vague mandate, but also one that permitted great flexibility.

A Strictly Canadian Affair: CURB's Operations

The day we decided to form CURB there were no American Ukrainians at the meeting. It was strictly a Canadian Ukrainian affair. And Canadians, in fact, carried the load for almost a year—from the end of 1945 through 1946—before the American Ukrainians really got involved. They gave us some money after CURB was established and after UCC in Winnipeg pressured them into doing so. Formally, UUARC agreed to share the budget, fifty-fifty, with UCC. But at the start it was strictly Canadian Ukrainian efforts that got things going. And it was the same people, more or less, who had set up and run UCSA's London club, the same facilities and the same executive personnel.

By this time things were happening quite fast in Europe. Military government, as foreseen by the Allies, was supposed to be a short transition period. It was followed by four-power zones of occupation, with the idea that as soon as possible the local civilian population would be allowed to take over their own management. It happened within a few short months in France, Belgium and Holland. But in Germany and Austria it couldn't happen that way. They had been the enemy. So there the Allies established the CCG, the Control Commission for Germany. After the armies relinguished control, the CCG took over. This was taking place towards the end of 1946.

Stanley Frolick Arrives

Some time before UCSA disbanded in London there was a knock at the door and a fellow came in dressed in khaki—Captain Stanley W. Frolick. He had come over to London from Canada en route to taking a position with the CCG and had further training to do in London. Indeed two Canadian Ukrainians came over to work with CCG among the thousands of others attached to this new organization. Many of them were soldiers, people who resigned from the military government to stay with the CCG. They were happy in Europe and didn't want to go home. You could do that. You could apply and be discharged overseas. I could have taken my discharge from the RCAF overseas and joined the CCG or UNRRA. Any of us could have done that because they were recruiting all the time and needed people with experience in Europe. Service duty with the forces was a great asset.

The other Ukrainian who came over to work with the CCG was a fellow who titled himself as Bishop Urbanovitch, from Winnipeg. Both he and Frolick came to our club. The bishop claimed to have at least four or five parishes in his jurisdiction. He claimed to have several degrees. He was really a bit of a fake I think. For instance he pretended to be an army chaplain. Stan was not like that. Stan was young and very knowledgeable on Ukrainian matters. Before war broke out in 1939 he had been a student in West Ukraine, then occupied by Poland. There he had become active in the Ukrainian nationalist underground, the OUN. I understand that he just made it out of the Soviet Union before the Germans invaded. Unless I'm mistaken he made it out via Japan. Anyway, back in Canada during the war, he was linked to UNF and worked in Ottawa for the government. After the war he came overseas to be in the CCG. He wore a uniform, with the rank of Captain—CCG personnel had the appearance of military men in order to make the German population feel that this was a continuity of the authority that had just defeated them and now ruled over them. So Stan Frolick came to England. He was to take further training as a translator and specialist in eastern European and Soviet affairs in London, as was Urbanovitch. Then they were both to go on to Germany. So his intention was to finish his course, mostly a Russian-language course, I believe, taught by the School of Slavonic and East European Studies, University of London. But they were almost daily visitors at UCSA. At first they lived in the club, but later this became inconvenient, so they moved to private quarters.

So when all this stuff with the Ukrainian refugees was beginning to mount and we got together and founded CURB with Stan Frolick's participation and I became the director, Stan the secretary and Peter Smylski became deputy director, we said, "Who's going to do the work here on the spot?" I was going back to Germany. So we said Stan Frolick was the man. He knew the Ukrainian language perfectly, he worked well with us as a friend and as part of a team. So we persuaded Stan to abandon his CCG work and to work for us full-time. He was interested. So he became the general secretary for CURB. We let him live in our building now and tried to get UCC to give us additional funds so we could pay him a small salary. All this was minimal. We wanted him to stay there and act as a pivot and pillar for CURB. (It must be recognized and appreciated, and I want to be the first to do so, that Stan Frolick's voluntary resignation from CCG, giving up an international military career for the very insecure, uncertain and low paying position he got in CURB, was an act of true devotion to the Ukrainian cause. After all, the rest of us had each completed a period of military service which, regardless of how long or how glorious or insignificant, was, nevertheless, acknowledged with a certificate of honourable service and medals of recognition. He would get none of this. Instead he was being asked to give up a career, after only a few short months overseas. It was an act of sacrifice on his part which should be recorded.)

We took one of the rooms in our Sussex Gardens building and just put a sign on the door—CURB—so that we wouldn't mix UCSA with CURB. We organized a new set of files for CURB. The relief work was growing and growing fast. We needed daily clerical help. So we hired an English girl to do our English typing, and we found a Mrs. Kowakska who could do our Ukrainian typing. I found a Ukrainian typewriter in a second-hand store which I bought and we already had an English typewriter from UCSA, so we were bilingual. We started doing all sorts of things. Stan came in daily. By then UNRRA had established its teams on the Continent. International relief work was moving apace very quickly. How rapidly could we deploy to take care of our Ukrainian DPs?

One of the first big jobs we tackled was a monumental thing really. It was a stupid thing looking at it now with hindsight, but we did it and it served its purpose. We drew up a small questionnaire, and we thought we could register every Ukrainian refugee or DP in western Europe. Monumental! We thought that there would be thousands, perhaps five to ten thousand. Actually it turned out that there were more than a million. Nobody at that time, when the war ended, really realised how many Ukrainians there were. I don't think we still do. But now I think there must have been about 2½ million—at least one million of whom were repatriated or who went back voluntarily to Ukraine, and about 35,000-40,000 of whom eventually ended up as immigrants to Canada. Other hundreds of thousands went to the United States and God knows where, all over the free world.[1] These are just off-the-cuff estimates, but I think pretty close to the truth.

Much was happening. Everyone was running around and so were we. Sending memoranda in defence of these Ukrainian DPs everywhere, running protests against forcible repatriation, getting Mrs. Roosevelt involved in saving our DPs, all while setting up the AUGB and continental Ukrainian relief committees. All these activities centred around our London office. So 218 Sussex Gardens was humming again. And I was the communications channel on the Continent, as were others. Sergeant George Luckyj was with the British Army of Occupation on the Rhine. He was one of our links there. All our contacts meant that we could monitor developments quickly, report back on them to North America and do whatever we could to ameliorate conditions on the spot. We were kept very busy!

The Ukrainian Canadian Veterans' Association

But our concerns were not solely tied to the Ukrainian DPs. We were thinking of what the future of our UCSA would be in Canada. Could we keep that wartime camaraderie and unity going there?

1. Scholarly descriptions of the post-World War Two refugee problem are provided in Malcolm Proudfoot, *European Refugees, 1939-1952: a Study in*

To try, we started the Ukrainian Canadian Veterans' Association (UCVA) early in 1945. An appointed committee, consisting of repatriated UCSA members or executive officers—like Ludwig Wojcichowsky (Kaye), John Yuzyk, Steve Kalin and John Karasevich—formed it. Because Capt. Karasevich lived in Winnipeg, he became our key man in UCVA and represented us to UCC. These UCVA representatives' job was to set up a Canadian Ukrainian veterans' organization which would help look after the welfare, repatriation and rehabilitation of our own soldiers back home. We were all young men and women going back—some to school, others to work, some were cripples and needed help and so on. This was a problem which the older generation of Ukrainians in Canada hadn't foreseen or faced up to earlier. They were more interested in Ukraine and in the liberation of Ukraine and the refugees. But who cared about the fellows who were returning from service overseas? Yet we had been the ones who had proven to Canada and the empire that our people were loyal citizens of this country.

Under pressure from us, UCC formed an additional committee in Winnipeg—a veterans' rehabilitation committee. The head of that committee was a lawyer, now judge, John R. Solomon. That was the beginning of UCVA. This transplanting of UCSA from England to Canada, there to be known as UCVA, was a gradual process from early 1945 through 1946. It was a funnelling of people from the one to the other and a restructuring of their organizational affiliations. Eventually we even sent all our UCSA documents and files to Canada.

UCVA started publishing a magazine called *Opinion*—a continuation of our *UCSA Newsletter*—and for a while it worked, but it started to flounder. The only reason that UCVA was functioning at all was because there was a bunch of veterans in Winnipeg, who were still collecting postwar benefits. They were getting paid for jobs. They were setting up businesses, going to school, some of them were setting up Canadian Legion branches. A group of them, for instance, got together and organized a delivery mail service called Spitfire Service. They were running around Win-

---

Forced Population Movement (London: Faber and Faber Ltd, 1957); and in Jacques Vernant, *The Refugee in the Post-War World* (New Haven, Conn.: Yale University Press, 1953).

nipeg on motorcycles. They were still young. But to get to solid things, to organize the grass roots, to form branches of UCVA and so on in the field, there was no one. UCC did not keep its end of the bargain. They stopped financing UCVA field workers, and the organization of our veterans in Canada came to a halt by mid-1946. Instead several Ukrainian branches of the Royal Canadian Legion were formed, registered and chartered in Montreal, Toronto, Hamilton, St. Catharines, Winnipeg and Edmonton. One UCVA branch was registered and chartered in Windsor. UCVA cells were formed, but not registered anywhere formally (except, of course, with UCVA headquarters) in Ottawa, Oshawa, Sudbury, London, Niagara Falls, Kingston, Dauphin, Saskatoon, Prince Albert, Lethbridge, Calgary, Vegreville, Vancouver and a few other places. Nothing more happened until I came back from England later in 1946.

So while CURB was growing in London, UCVA was setting up in Winnipeg and UCSA was gradually petering out—all in this transition period, 1945-46. CURB, meanwhile, was taking under its wing both European Ukrainian relief committees and various Ukrainian groups in places like Argentina and Brazil. Every relief committee which existed or which we thought should exist we put on our CURB letterhead. And as soon as they were formed, or in the process of being formed, we'd give them a letter signed by Frolick and myself saying, for example, "This is to certify that the Ukrainian Relief Committee in Belgium is affiliated with CURB and any assistance and cooperation that you can provide them with would be sincerely appreciated." We did that in Rome with Bishop Buchko, in Paris, anywhere and with anybody who wanted to form a relief committee. Anybody who wanted CURB's help was welcome to it. And by that time, we saw that we also needed a body in England at least on paper. So I made a trip to Manchester and we founded a relief committee in Britain. Michael Cannon became the president, Lesniowsky was the secretary. I don't think that during its period of existence they wrote more than ten letters, if that. At this time the Division was still in Rimini and there were EVWs coming into England under the "Westward Ho" schemes and the AUGB was running its own show. So the old community in Manchester and their social club became somewhat redundant and unnecessary. But in the transition we needed them on paper.

84

All this time I was travelling around Europe visiting the DP camps. I saw them grow from small groups of people to camps with three, four, five thousand people in them. So it is very hard to generalize about the DP camps. Camp organization and administration depended very much on which occupation zone it was in. The Americans, for instance, turned over everything to UNRRA and gave it a free hand pretty well. The British preferred to keep all authority and responsibility in the hands of the military government, but gave the refugees inside the DP camps a relatively free hand.

The question of Ukrainian identity was one of the earliest problems. Who, the authorities wondered, were these Ukrainians? Were they Soviet citizens who should be repatriated, or Poles who should be placed in Polish DP camps, or were they a separate people? The small camps which sprang up spontaneously generally in the centres where these people were employed (munitions factories, military bases, etc.) had to be merged to facilitate the logistic needs of management and control. Certain camps would be liquidated, their inhabitants moved about. And what about the political disturbances becoming so evident? In some cases people had to be separated. Sometimes even Ukrainians from the different regions had to be segregated. Lysenko DP camp, near Hannover, was a big problem. It was a political hotbed—West Ukrainians against East Ukrainians, Orthodox against Catholic, OUN Revolutionaries (OUNr) versus OUN Solidarists (OUNs) and so on.

Sometimes a lot of our people started as a sub-camp, a suburb camp of a Polish one because there were more Poles locally, or as a sub-camp of a Baltic one. Gradually they wanted to be by themselves. It varied. In the camps where there were Ukrainians in a majority, the largest number of them weren't political emigrants, just plain uprooted humanity. The political refugees were those who claimed that the whole diaspora was a political emigration, that this was the difference between this one and the interwar emigration to Canada. The political refugees were largely to be found in the last stream who came into Germany and Austria from the East. They were literally moving out of Ukraine at the last moment just in front of the Soviets. Some UPA groups even managed to get out as late as the fall of 1947.[1] A lot of them were ardent nationalists and violently anti-communist. But the majority of those who were in Germany and Austria earlier, were slave workers and DPs, only relatively few of whom were political. Of this latter type most were those who were emigré politicians from the World War One years, like Hetman Pavlo Skoropadsky, Prof. Kubijovych, the Ukrainian Republican government supporters who had been based in Warsaw. These people had felt that it was necessary to get to the West, there to proclaim the Ukrainian cause. They ended up in territories overrun by the Germans during World War Two. Some believed German lies that they would free Ukraine from the Soviets. Later, of course, other political refugees got out to the West. I've mentioned the UPA already. There were also the OUN cadres. Well, there were other groups of theirs who were sent out as emissaries to Italy in late 1943, and some were sent to Spain towards the end of the war. For these people, one way or another, it was possible to travel to other countries via an organized Ukrainian underground.

One incident I know of is how two UPA and UHVR emissaries got through to Spain, where, unfortunately, the Spanish authorities got suspicious about them. Spain was supposedly neutral. Yet these Ukrainians, thought to be agents of some power, were arrested and put in jail in Madrid just at the time the war had ended. There was a big conference of the *Pax Romana* organization in London, a strong, Catholic international organization. There were delegations from all of the countries that were free and able to send someone. There was a big delegation from Spain. Through our own network of informants we learned about these two fellows who were arrested in Madrid. So Joe Ramanov, Stan Frolick and Father Horoshko went to the *Pax Romana* conference as "delegates from Canada," all in uniform. They were to establish contact with the Spanish delegates at the conference, which they did. They had a conversation and told them, "Do you know that you

_____

1. On October 1, 1947 the Toronto *Globe and Mail* carried a front-page article regarding the penetration of the Iron Curtain by UPA groups heading from East to West. UPA carried on active guerilla resistance against Soviet occupation until the mid-1950s.

are holding two nice Ukrainian Catholics as prisoners, men who shouldn't be imprisoned? What are you going to do about it?" They were surprised, but they agreed to do something. So within a matter of a week, the two of them were released. One of them is still living, Karmanin, who married Olya Kowbel, now in Toronto. He was one of those UPA soldiers who was sent out of Ukraine to establish contact with the West.

CURB's biggest asset was that we were organized, that we had an active group of people, that we thought we knew where we were going, that we were open, sincere and frank. Not only during the war, but certainly after it and during the entire Canadian Ukrainian relief operation up until 1952 when I came back to Canada, our efforts were largely taken up with lobbying. You know, meeting the right people, trying to persuade them to recognize the unique nature of the Ukrainian DP problem, arguing that they do something, whether it was to release Ukrainians from prisons or to straighten out camp arrangements, or to transfer somebody from one DP camp to another, or to make available certain supplies to a person in hospital, or, later on, to admit immigrants. That was CURB's main job. Let me give you one example. Australia and New Zealand had never really heard of Ukrainians before 1945. We went to the doors of their embassies, met their high commissioners in London, set up conferences with their senior officials and tried to sell them on the idea that they should accept Ukrainian immigrants. Today in Australia and New Zealand we have twenty to thirty thousand Ukrainian immigrants. A new community in the Ukrainian diaspora was opened up; the same thing in Britain where we had twelve to fifteen families to start with, and where there is now a settlement of over 30,000. The same is true for South America. We helped place our DPs everywhere possible.

We also got supplies to UPA. We did that in various stages and in various forms—cigarettes and CARE parcels. I can only speak about those things with which I was closely concerned, but one thing that I recall—it was shortly after we had entered Germany and liberated Bergen-Belsen concentration camp in the British Zone, the Germans were retreating quickly. We established our RCAF air base at Celle near Soltau. Our mission was to go into Bergen-Belsen and bring in blankets, foodstuffs and medical supplies. I was one of the officers involved because I was in intelligence. There were seven of us. But I was the only Ukrainian and interested in Ukrainians primarily. Two people with whom I became closely associated were prisoners in this camp—Roman Spolsky and Kosarenko-Kosarevich, an East Ukrainian and a Ukrainian National Republic supporter already in his fifties. Spolsky had been in the UPA, was an OUNr follower, a young boy of twenty-four or twenty-five or so. He told me confidentially that in the Carpathian Mountains, UPA had a field hospital and they needed medical supplies. I believed his plea was genuine. Well, I certainly couldn't give him any official help from the Canadian authorities or military, but one thing that I could do was give him all kinds of cigarette parcels from Canada and I could get more whenever I wanted them from our club in London just on request. Cigarettes then were worth their weight in gold in Germany. There were two staples in postwar Europe, worth more than dollars— cigarettes and soap. You could get anything for these items, do anything. And so we organized a small operation whereby I handed over thousands of cigarettes to Spolsky, he sold them for supplies which then went to UPA. UPA wanted to stay in Ukraine and fight, hoping their ranks would be re-inforced with help from the West. That was their hope—of course, the West never really came to their aid.

The other operation with which we were concerned was about a year later in 1947, after a UPA contingent broke through to our side in Germany. IRO rules prohibited anyone who was a political activist from being sheltered under the refugee label, or admitted to a DP camp. So all UPA soldiers presented us with a special case. What to do with them? Certainly IRO wouldn't take them. So we organized our own relief for them, an operation whereby we gave them CARE parcels. By that time—and this is where the American Ukrainians were way ahead of us—UUARC had direct relations with CARE, and they could get almost unlimited parcels for any specific purpose that Dr. Gallan, as head, would sanction. CARE would do it. The Canadian Ukrainians had no link with CARE. There were many cases in which these American Ukrainians were able to make arrangements superior to our own; they had good links in their own zone, for example. And I suppose it had a lot to do with the fact that UUARC became such a big operation in Europe, whereas the Canadian Ukrainian operation was much smaller.

Anyway, we gave these UPA people CARE parcels, then we distributed them among Ukrainian DP camps. Finally they were accorded DP status and were allowed to stay in camps, recognized as refugees. But before that happened we gave them a lot of parcels and carried them for a while as our own responsibility.

I Return to Canada

The RCAF, by this time, was insisting that I go back to Canada because they could not keep me in Europe any longer. It was time to repatriate me to Canada. The alternative—to take my discharge overseas—I decided I just wouldn't do for many reasons. I was married and I had an elderly, widowed mother living alone in Canada. So I kept on pressing UCC in Winnipeg to send somebody to take over CURB permanently, and the only reply that I got from them was "you stay." My wife and I had decided we were going back to Canada. I must admit, I felt very guilty about leaving the Ukrainian DPs. I would have felt equally perturbed if I had stayed there. I had to start thinking about having a normal life with my wife, who was also still in the forces and due for repatriation. It was a question of being repatriated at some later date to Canada, but at our own expense, or returning now at government expense. We did not have much money. I was not going to take my discharge overseas, which UCC insisted I do. They pleaded with us to stay overseas, but if we took our discharge there, who would pay for the return trip to Canada, whenever that came about? With my mother alone in Saskatoon, we wanted to take advantage of the Canadian government's commitment to bring home all its troops—we were entitled to that. So we talked Stan Frolick into staying on to look after things in CURB. We promised to support him in Canada as much as we could and above all to see that more help was sent to him.

My wife and I came back to Canada in May 1946 on the *Queen Elizabeth*. We were among the last troops to be repatriated. We landed in Quebec and went through the first stage of demobilization in Montreal. Then, on the way back to Saskatoon we stopped in Toronto, Fort William and Winnipeg, where we were discharged. Local Ukrainian groups and UCC put on receptions for us in all these places because I was the "returning hero," so to speak. When we got to Winnipeg we had a long meeting with the Ukrainian Canadian Committee. It is all recorded in their minutes. They said that they were going to do something to continue the work I had started and done for the Ukrainian war victims in Europe, that they were going to "call a meeting." When they did they would call me in. In the meantime, I persuaded them that they should send some money to Frolick, serving as CURB's caretaker, because the budget was very limited. They sent another $2,000. We went back to Saskatoon, and I registered at the University of Saskatchewan for a summer course in history. In the meantime, F/L Joe Romanov had come back. So had Capt. Peter Smylski. They had done the same thing. They reported to Winnipeg. They had meetings with the Ukrainian Canadian Committee. They insisted on the same thing that I did. We all were doing the same thing, pleading for help because we were all members of the founding group of CURB and knew that UCC had to do something urgently to help CURB continue. I was resigned to the fact that this was the end of my overseas work. My heart was in it still, but I had a mother and wife to take care of.

UCVA's Growing Pains

In the meantime UCVA was beginning to grow with the number of returning veterans, and I pitched in. The UCVA executive planned a Canada-wide tour for me to organize UCVA branches and speak on the refugee problem. So I went into the field again, organizing branches and recruiting members throughout western Canada. We sent Tony Yaremovich to eastern Canada. Of course, wherever I went, I also told people about the Ukrainian DPs and helped popularize the issue among Canadian Ukrainians. Many had family members, relatives and friends in European DP camps. So people were eager for news. Others were also organizing UCSA—Steve Pawluk and others in Toronto; John Yuzyk must have covered all of Canada at least twice. This was to be a new Ukrainian organization in Canada. Unfortunately, I think it was seen as a threat to every other already established Canadian Ukrainian organization, although we never meant it to be. UNF felt it would draw away its members, so did USRL and BUC. They wanted the returning veterans to come back into the old organizations. They were sure that when Canadian Ukrainian servicemen came back they would

90

immediately return to the organizations of yester-year from which many of us had come. I would go back into the Orthodox groups, men like Romanow would go back to the Catholics and so on. But we veterans were not thinking that way. Here was a new organization and the resources the old ones had relied on were being lost to it. The old organizations never truly welcomed the formation of UCVA, nor did the UCC. That hindered UCVA work and limited its chances.

I still recall when they put on a reception for us in the P. Mohyla Institute in Saskatoon very shortly after returning to Canada—these were all former members of our Ukrainian Orthodox youth movement. There were about eight of us returnees there—Prociuk, Burianyk, myself and my wife, and a few others, all officers. I stood up and suggested to the audience that we were now coming to a new period in Canadian Ukrainian history characterized by two things: 1) that this was an era of unity and that all Ukrainians would have to pull together much more than before, developing some kind of *modus vivendi* for co-existence, and 2) that anybody who was fifty years old or older shouldn't run for office, in other words that this was an era for the young. Well, I got shot down in flames later, although in private. All I said was heresy. No one should promote such things. You had to be loyal to the traditions and backgrounds from which you came. There could be no unity with other Canadian Ukrainians. The problem of factionalism with Canadian Ukrainian circles was still very much alive. That depressed me. I remember writing to Frolick about it.

While I was happy in my little house at 1307 Alexandra Avenue in Saskatoon with my wife and mother, I was still troubled over the fate of our Ukrainian DPs. We had some chickens, a little garden and our house, and my wife and I settled down to life. But I couldn't sleep nights thinking of the refugees and the Division in Europe. Then I got a telegram from UCC around the middle of August 1946: "Will you come to a meeting?" So I went to this meeting in Winnipeg, a lot of our boys were there—among them Tony Yaremovich, John Karasevich, John Yuzyk and Ann Crapleve—and UCC said to me, "We want you to go back overseas." They had approached some people, some who had sat out the war and done nothing, but now had a lot to say in the Ukrainian Canadian community—people you meet in the streets now and who are embarrassed about what they did or did not do in the war. But they couldn't find anybody to send. UCC realized the scale of our Ukrainian refugee problem—Volodymyr Kossar, Rev. Sawchuk, Dr. Kushnir and all these people—were astute enough that way, and they knew it had to be dealt with. But who would UCC send over? Someone who had been there before would obviously be best suited. Now in part that made sense. People with experience of Europe, who had been involved, such as those of us who had formed CURB, knew what to expect and so on. But it didn't make sense from the point of view that the same individual or individuals should continue making personal sacrifices.

But it seemed there was no one else. They said point-blank to me, "We want you to go over again." When they made that serious request, we asked for an adjournment and we veterans pulled out and went to a little room by ourselves for a caucus. We drafted a memorandum to UCC, the first time likely that a Canadian Ukrainian organization had drafted a memorandum to this umbrella group—it was our UCVA "Renaissance Plan." In this memorandum we said basically that we believed that sending one person overseas was pointless. Forget about it, one Panchuk or anybody else was not enough. The job was too big, it was absolutely impossible. We had to be realistic. If the veterans who had been over there before were to go, yet again, they should get prepared to organize a mission, it would have to involve at least four to six or more staff and field people, depending on how many the community was willing and able to support. We would go back for one year. One year was the condition. Also we insisted that UCC spare no efforts here at home to organize groups of veterans (branches of UCVA). UCC had to promise to support that. And we got a number of our people together. We got Ludwig Kaye, who had been our UCSA secretary for a short while overseas. We got Steve Kalin who had been our historian overseas. We arranged that they go out into the field as UCC representatives. They would serve UCC while also setting up UCVA branches. They would help collect money for the refugee cause, for CURB, but at the same time they would build up a list of local veterans and organize them. They would be organizing UCVA, while building up UCC. We thought this was only fair, given what UCC expected from us overseas.

92

I want to repeat for emphasis why we felt so strongly about UCVA. We were enthused with our experiences in London at the club where we had joined Ukrainian Catholics and Orthodox, young and old, right and left, all together. We were carried away by that ideal situation, and we hoped that this could be put into practice in Winnipeg, Ottawa, Montreal, Toronto and so on, that we could establish similar peacetime clubs for our youth across Canada. We wanted to preserve our wartime unity, what rooted UCSA together, we wanted Canadian Ukrainian unity to intensify. We would work as a single Ukrainian Canadian community because the only thing that jelled the community was what we had done overseas. Prior to that the Ukrainian community here was only bickering and infighting. Instead of building more Orthodox buildings, more UNF halls and more Ukrainian Catholic centres, we wanted to see built united Ukrainian Canadian community centres right across the land. It was a philosophy for a new way of life and the Ukrainian community in Canada. We wished for a renaissance of Canadian Ukrainian life here. Possibly we were too idealistic.

But we did make the effort, those were the conditions in our memorandum to UCC. And they bought it. They agreed, one after another. And they said they were going to help finance the people who would go into the field to do this work for us, for UCVA. When they committed themselves, we said we'd go, and so the Canadian Relief Mission for Ukrainian War Victims was born.

I have a suspicion, with the wisdom of hindsight, that they were trying to get rid of us, kill two birds with one stone. Solve the problem of who to send back by sending us and nip the new UCVA organization in the bud. I may be doing them an injustice by saying this, and I certainly didn't think of it at the time, but the subsequent turn of events seems to indicate that that was the intention of our elders. That way they could maintain the strength of UNF, USRL and BUC, while letting UCVA flounder. Now I don't know for sure that this is how it happened. In my heart I don't think anybody was so Machiavellian as to have planned it all out that way. The subsequent events were likely coincidental. Yet I often wonder if our departure from Canada fitted into some peoples' plans. Johnny Yuzyk even wrote to me about this once, saying:

...the older leaders hate to see you getting so popular and also powerful.... I only want to mention that you do what you think best since you know the set in Europe and Canada better than I ever will. All I know is that you are my friend and I'd hate to see you get the old run around by some of our scheming friends. [Some within UCC may have felt] the best move [was] to keep you in Europe (sort of out of the way).

Rumours floating around Canada had it that I was giving preference to Orthodox refugees, being Orthodox myself. Presumably, I would be doling out more relief supplies their way, or something. Of course, that was nonsense. All of us helped all Ukrainian refugees, whoever they were. Still, some Ukrainian Catholics, shortly after our return overseas in 1946, did start their separate relief work, headed by Bishop Ladyka. Almost simultaneously some Catholic veterans in Canada, for unknown reasons, cooled towards UCVA, except in three legion branches (Toronto, Winnipeg and Edmonton) where they crawled into their "Canadian" shell and retreated from anything and everything too Ukrainian. What could we do about it? Nothing. We just kept working. But UCVA, in Canada, never really made it. We were abandoned here while some of our best workers were overseas helping the DPs.

The UCC Mistrusts Frolick

The leading people in UCC (Kushnir, Sawchuk, Kossar) were upset at this time about the news regarding Frolick's actions as interim head of CURB more than I was. I did not know that much. During that short interval from my return to Saskatoon to my departure for Europe again, in late 1946, the UCC was getting copies of correspondence and letters, even from Dr. Gallan, that I only saw afterwards. The one who was most disturbed in UCC was Kossar, president of UNF, because he was learning that Frolick was a UHVR and OUN Revolutionaries supporter, whereas the UNF had supported the OUN Solidarists of Colonel Melnyk. Kossar was himself a top *Melnykivtsi,* and at that time this rift in the OUN was a very, very hot potato since early 1940. UNF information was that Frolick was using CURB to run an underground movement for the *Banderivtsi.* Kossar and Kushnir felt that something had to be done to stop this urgently. Kossar was anxious that I should go back because he knew me, my record and that I did not support the OUN Revolutionaries—I would run CURB for humanitarian relief purposes and follow UCC policy.

The Canadian Relief Mission for Ukrainian Victims of War

When I was asked to organize the UCRF's mission returning to England, and to head it, I agreed. I could only do so on the basis of people who were willing and able to go on a voluntary basis. Of course, my wife stood beside me. Tony Yaremovich was not married, so he was willing to have another go at Europe for a year while postponing his return to university. John Karasevich definitely was not going to go. He was already registered at the University of Manitoba and finishing his law degree. The Worobetz boys weren't going. None of quite a few people we contacted were willing to go back. They were either too settled or too resettled to again disrupt their lives—they wouldn't go.

So the only people I could get were my wife, Tony Yaremovich, Ann Crapleve (still a single girl who had worked like a beaver in UCSA and was one of the main pillars of our organization during the war). The four of us went back. It was in October 1946. We were the Canadian Relief Mission for Ukrainian Refugees (and War Victims). The name was suggested to us by Dr. V.J. Kaye who was then working in the Department of National War Services in Ottawa. He saw how government people acted and reacted to Canadian Ukrainian affairs in Ottawa. He was very anxious that we should not make our mission too Ukrainian because it would "smell" of politics. So we covered it as much as possible in a purely Canadian garb. He even advised that when we were back in London we should help CURB as much as possible, but keep CURB and our mission separate and address as much mail as possible to Canada House. That would appear Canadian and quell any residual doubts about our intentions. So we had letterhead printed, and our badges read "Canadian Relief Mission for Ukrainian Refugees." Then when we visited and stayed in military barracks, we were there as Canadians, for a special job to help Ukrainians. We were *always* having to downplay any overly Ukrainian connection because at this time the West was still very sensitive to Soviet complaints about Ukrainian agitation—against repatriation, against the Soviet Union and so on. If we got branded as a political mission instead of a welfare group, we'd be hampered in what we could do. Europe was closed to all except those recognized by the authorities.

After we had agreed on the terms of our mission with UCC, the question of finances was raised. We were so young, so naive, so unrealistic that we said, "We don't want any pay, we'll go voluntarily, we have certain grants and benefits that we collected as a result of having served in the armed forces. That is enough for us as long as you pay day-to-day expenses—the cost of transportation, food, etc. No salary. Nothing at all." The only thing we asked for ourselves was the minimal amount of $50 each per month for personal expenditures. We agreed to that and they agreed to it, and that was that. We left for England.

Stan Frolick was still holding the fort in London, waiting to see what would happen. Either someone was going to come as director of the bureau, or someone was going to send him money and make him director. He was the only executive member left there with his two secretaries and George Kluchevsky as treasurer. Helping Stan out in his work were Joe Ratushniak, Bill Byblow and Danylo Skoropadsky. CURB was still actively working. Before we had left England for Canada, we had found two Ukrainian students, D. Martinowsky (later a professor at St. Andrew's College, Winnipeg) and George (Finlay) Kluchevsky, who became CURB's treasurer when Ann Crapleve first was discharged and returned to Canada, to help us out; and they were still there pending reinforcements from Canada.

Frolick's Activities within CURB: the Controversy

When we returned to London, we found a bit of chaos at 218 Sussex Gardens. As I've said before we left there had been this Association of Ukrainian Soldiers in the Polish Armed Forces which had been given a basement room in our building for their headquarters. Their key man was Petro Pihichyn, a very ardent OUNr supporter. I didn't know it at that time, but it seems he was deeply involved in the Ukrainian nationalist underground. There were others as well. Some of them had got to England with the Polish forces, others as EVWs, some were on the Continent and Stan had close contact with them. Between them (Frolick and Pihichyn)—and I think both (objectively speaking) were acting in good faith—each thought that he was doing the best thing that

96

Cartoon of Panchuk, as drawn by Ukrainian SEP at Rimini for their camp newspaper *Wasp*, 13 April 1947

Bohdan Panchuk's parents: Mychailo (1862-1915) and Maria (1887-1956)

The UCSA Services Club at 218 Sussex Gardens, London; officially opened at UCSA Ukrainian Easter Get-Together, 15 April 1944; later served as headquarters for CURB

UCSA Ukrainian Christmas Get-Together and First Anniversary Meeting, 6-7 January 1944; UCSA executive (left to right) front row: Lieut. Walter Kupchenko, Cpl. Ann Crapleve, P/O Bohdan Panchuk, L/Cpl. Helen Kozicky, Pte. Joe Choma (in civilian clothes) back row: Cpl. Steve Kalin; F/L Joe Kohut, DFC; LAC Alex Kreptul; F/O Adam Pohoreski

Typical UCSA office scene, 1944 (left to right): LAC John Yuzyk, LAW Anne Cherniawsky, UCSA president Bohdan Panchuk and CWAC Helen Kozicky

Two UCSA chaplains and the vicar (from left to right): Rev. S. Sawchuk; the vicar, Rev. G.T. Chappell; and Rev. Michael Horoshko, 1944

Our seventh UCSA Get-Together to celebrate Mother's Day and Ukrainian Easter, 5 May 1945; Ukrainians from Manchester were honoured as special guests; at far left, Danylo Skoropadsky and Lady Hill; seated near centre left are Helen Kozicky, the club director, and Mrs. Solar; at far right, wearing glasses, is Mr. Lesniowsky, secretary of the Ukrainian Social Club in Manchester

UCSA flag presented to the Ukrainian Canadian servicemen by Belgian Ukrainian refugees at a Brussels Get-Together, November 1945

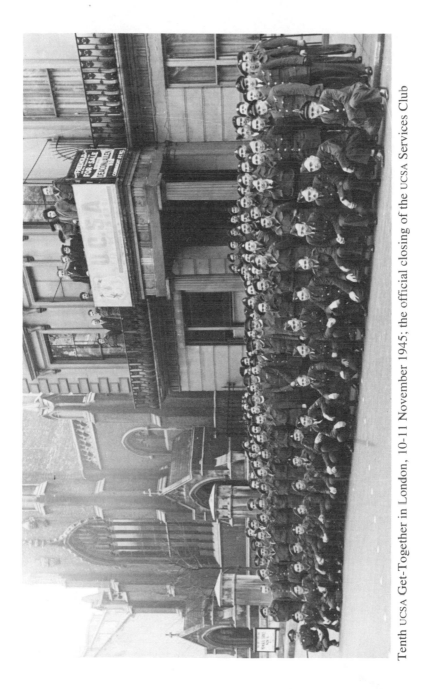

Tenth UCSA Get-Together in London, 10-11 November 1945; the official closing of the UCSA Services Club

Presentations at tenth UCSA Get-Together, 10-11 November 1945 (left to right): F/L Bohdan Panchuk, Sgt. Anthony Yaremovich, Capt. M. Lucyk, Capt. Rev. Symchych and Capt. Peter Smylski

Ukrainian Christmas Get-Together, 5-6 January 1946; head table (left to right): Capt. S.W. Frolick, Capt. Peter Smylski, Rev. B. Kushnir (UCC president), F/L Bohdan Panchuk, Sgt. Anthony Yaremovich and Capt. B. Mychaly-shyn; at right (front) Danylo Skoropadsky and Lady Hill

Wedding of Bohdan Panchuk and Anne Cherniawsky, London, 2 February 1946 (left to right): Capt. S. Davidovich, Capt. A.M. Homik, Capt. S.W. Frolick, Capt. D. Melnyk, Capt. Walter Grenkow and Capt. Peter Smylski; Bestman F/L J. Romanow, Maid of Honour LAW E. Winarski

Some UCSA and CURB members in London, 1946 (left to right): F/L Bohdan Panchuk, Capt. Peter Smylski, F/L Joseph Romanow, George Kluchevsky and S.W. Frolick (Courtesy of S.W. Frolick)

PCIRO meeting in Geneva, 1947; Panchuk (centre) consults with (left to right) Dr. Waddams and Peter Molson

Canada was represented at the PCIRO meeting by Ambassador Jean Desy

DP camp at Heidenau (left to right): Capt. Michael Kapusta, Capt. Rev. S.P. Symchych and Capt. S. W. Frolick, 13 January 1946 (Courtesy of S. W. Frolick)

The Panchuks visiting the Ukrainian SEP camp in Rimini, spring 1947

Joint Ukrainian Catholic and Ukrainian Orthodox liturgical celebration in Rimini, 1947

Canadian Relief Mission for Ukrainian Refugees, London, October 1946 (left to right) front row: Anne Cherniawsky, Bill Byblow, Ann Crapleve back row: Bohdan Panchuk, Michael Krysowaty, Anthony Yaremovich

Panchuk with Metropolitan Polikarp of the Ukrainian Greek Orthodox Church in Paris, 1947

Belgium's Ukrainian Relief Committee (left to right): unidentified man, Hanka Romanchych (a Canadian), Dmytro Andrievsky and Mykola Hrab

Capt. Stanley W. Frolick en route to a Military Government detachment at Aurich near Oldenburg, December 1945 (Courtesy of S.W. Frolick)

Ann Crapleve, BEM, 1945 (Courtesy of Mrs. Ann Smith (Crapleve))

Ann Crapleve, director of UCRF operations in Germany, greeting Mr. and Mrs. Eustace Wasylyshen, Bielefeld, 1 April 1949 (Courtesy of Mrs. Anne Wasylyshen)

Ukrainian RED CROSS in Geneve-
Suisse
1. Place du Grand Menzel, 1.

Committee: ....

Certificate

Bescheinigung

Ukrainisches Rotes Kreuz in Genf

Zweigstelle: ....

N. .... Date ....

Mr. (Mrs., Miss) ....

.... Ukrainian

born ....

in ....

confession ....

nationality ....

....

fami'y position ....

occupation ....

    The Ukrainian Red Cross in Geneva
takes care for the bearer of this certificate.

....
Representative

COMITÉ INTERNATIONAL DE LA CROIX-ROUGE
DÉLEGATION AU CANADA

ERNEST L. MAAG
DELEGATE

MONTREAL, **October 11,1946.**
1040 SUN LIFE BUILDING

<u>TO WHOM IT MAY CONCERNS</u>

    The bearer of this, Mr. G.R.B. Panchuk, M.B.E. Director of the
RELIEF MISSION TO UKRAINIAN REFUGEES and DISPLACED PERSONS in Europe, is
member of a team sponsored by the UKRAINIAN CANADIAN VETERANS ASSOCIATIONS,
by the UKRAINIAN CANADIAN COMMITTEE and the UKRAINIAN CANADIAN RELIEF FUND,
consisting of:

                Himself as Director,
                Mr. A.J. Yaremovich, Asst-Director,
                Miss Ann Crapleve, B.E.M. Secretary-treasurer,
                Mrs. Anne Panchuk, Welfare Officer.

    This team is interested in the alleviation of the living conditions
of the Displaced Persons of Ukrainian origin and acts on behalf of the Ukrainian Canadian Relief Fund which is authorized in Canada by the Department
of the National War Services.

    The undersigned would personally appreciate any assistance that may
be given to Mr. Panchuk and the other members of his team in the exercise
of his relief work amongst Ukrainians in Europe.

                Delegate in Canada of the
           INTERNATIONAL COMMITTEE OF THE RED CROSS

UKRAINIAN CANADIAN SERVICEMEN'S ASSOCIATION
(ACTIVE SERVCE OVERSEAS)
218 SUSSEX GARDENS, PADDINGTON, LONDON, W.2.

CIRCULAR LETTER No. 21　　　　　　　　　　　TEL.: PADDINGTON 2029

Dear Servicemen,　　　　　　　　　　　　　*September 30th 1945.*

1. ENCLOSURES.

Enclosed with this Circular are the following :—

DONATED BY G. R. B. PANCHUK

(a) The latest issue of our Newsletter, Issue No. 10
(b) A sample souvenir copy of the U.C.S.A. postcard
(c) A sample copy of the U.C.S.A. Xmas card

With regard to these enclosures, please note that most postcards and Xmas cards can be obtained from the U.C.S.A. office at threepence each.

With regard to the Newsletter, your attention is particularly drawn to the Editorial, the article on Christian Citizenship Training, and the Messages from our Padres. Your comments, suggestions and criticisms with regard to the Newsletter would be sincerely appreciated.

2. UKRAINIAN-CANADIAN VETERANS' COMMITTEE.

As has been announced, an Initiative Committee of our Veterans Association has already been formed. It is the purpose and intention of this Veterans' Committee to try and lay the foundation of our future Veterans organization, which, as is now the case with our Servicemen's Association, will unite together all Ukrainian Canadian Veterans of this war. The Committee is working together and in co-operation with the Canadian Legion with all other Veteran organizations and with all our Ukrainian organizations.

The final constitution will likely be announced at our first large Get-Together that we will have when we all get back to Canada. In the meantime it is most vital and important that we have as complete a list as possible of all those Ukrainian Canadians who have served in this war.

Recently there appeared in all the Ukrainian papers in Canada, an appeal from our Veterans' Committee addressed to all Veterans and those soon about to be Veterans. We want to take this opportunity to endorse this appeal whole heartedly, and again wish to remind all our members to send their own names and home addresses, and the names and home addresses of any of their Ukrainian friends in the forces to the following address :-

Ukrainian-Canadians Veterans' Committee,
715 McIntyre Building, Winnipeg, Man., Canada.

3. HISTORICAL QUESTIONNAIRE No. 3.

The Questionnaire that we sent out with our last Circular Letter is for the purpose of helping us compile the history of our united Ukrainian Canadian war effort. A considerable number of these Questionnaires have been filled and returned, but that is only a small percentage of those we sent out. We again appeal to one and all of you not only to fill our Questionnaires and to return them to us, but also to keep sending us every name that you can possibly find of Ukrainians in the Armed Forces. If you send us the names we will take all necessary action to contact the individuals, to send them literature and to introduce them to our organization, but we must have more names. At the same time, we would also remind all our members that when sending the Questionnaire, a personal photo (portrait) is required if at all possible; failing a photo, even a snapshot is better than nothing at all.

4. CENTRAL UKRAINIAN RELIEF BUREAU.

⯈ Under the joint auspices of the Ukrainian Canadian Relief Fund, which is an Auxiliary of the Canadian Red Cross, and the United Ukrainian American Relief Committee, Incorporated, Authorised by the President's War Relief Control Board, there has been opened in the same building as our Club, a Central Relief Bureau. The purpose of the Bureau in brief is to extend any and every moral and material aid possible on behalf of the Sponsoring Committees, to all Ukrainian Refugees, Displaced Persons and destitute on the Continent.

P.T.O.

could be done for the Ukrainian cause. And I still would never take that away from them. They started publishing things on our CURB Gestetner machine, news and information, some of which was not really honest or true. Maybe they had no way of checking it out. News was planted. I was slightly aware of this, and I knew there were dangers. My policy, my intention was, although I'm interested, let's not touch the political aspect—not touch anything that's really deeply political or partisan. Let's stick to the humanitarian saving of lives. Otherwise we'll get in trouble with the authorities, without whose support we can't really operate. That's all we have to do, save one or two million lives, we don't know how many. Let's stick to that and do nothing else. The rest will come in its own time.

It so happened that after we'd been back about two weeks, I don't know how it happened, but by mistake, we got a whole package of correspondence, which wasn't intended for us. It was all pure underground, UPA, UHVR, OUNr material, including orders to representatives in the field, instructions on what they should do and so on. We confronted Stan Frolick with it since it was totally contrary to previous CURB policy of not getting embroiled in Ukrainian political party work. Later, this was on the 28 of November 1946, I wrote to Dr. Kaye from London saying, "When a thing has reached such a state that it scares us to think what might have happened if we had not come when we did. Not only was he [Stan Frolick] setting up political propaganda, but we have definite proof now that at the same time when he was holding the position at the Bureau—to all intents and purposes a civil service job so far as UCC was concerned—he also accepted a position as the UK representative of the general secretary of UHVR (Ukrainian Supreme Liberation Council)." This was in that package of mail we had, and Frolick was giving instructions, he was running the show in the United Kingdom. I suppose you could call him the UHVR's resident in England with direct links to Mykola Lebed and Stepan Bandera.[1] It was at this time, likely when he got over to Munich (before I originally left for Canada) that he got the idea

---

1. Stepan Bandera, leader of the OUN Revolutionaries, headed up this powerful Ukrainian emigré nationalist movement until his assassination by a Soviet agent in Munich, on October 15, 1959.

to eventually publish a newspaper in Canada. *Homin Ukrainy* (Echo of Ukraine) can be traced back to these days.

Anyway, Frolick's sympathies were all with the UHVR and OUN—that is Bandera movement contacts. At that time we didn't know, but that's the way it turned out. They founded the Ukrainian Information Bureau, I think they called it. It was all stuff that was purely UHVR, UPA and narrow party political stuff. Nobody knew anything else. I only knew what his general feelings were overseas before I went back to Canada in 1946. It was interesting because I was learning too. As I've said, Frolick had been near Lviv when war broke out in 1939, and he got involved with OUN, which I never knew anything about and I wasn't aware of until after the war, when these troubles surfaced in CURB.

We told Stan now, "This cannot go on. It has to stop." Frolick couldn't buy it, and Pihichyn didn't have to buy it. But we offered Frolick the opportunity. We said, "Join our mission. There are four of us. You can be the fifth. Let's work together and we'll have five instead of four." He was already discharged and living in England. He took the stand that this was somehow an act of distrust, perhaps a show of no confidence in him. I don't know how he took it. About the time that I had returned to Canada and when deliberations were going on in Winnipeg as to whom to send over as director of CURB to take my place, Dr. Gallan, the executive director of UUARC in Philadelphia, which was also helping finance CURB, had arrived in London on a fact-finding visit to western Europe to see for himself the things he in fact already knew from our reports.

When it appeared that I wasn't coming back and Stan felt that he was in charge, Gallan (there are letters about that) said, "Well, we cannot operate like this in mid-air. If we are going to give money, we [the UUARC] are going to have more to say." And I think he appointed Stan Frolick as the director of CURB. UCC (Kushnir, Kossar and everybody) felt that Dr. Gallan had overstepped his jurisdiction by doing this. The whole relief program had been a Canadian Ukrainian thing to start with, although UUARC was sharing the budget for half a year or so—the relief work to this time had been done solely and exclusively by us Canadians.

Stan insisted that Dr. Gallan had appointed him director of CURB. Dr. Gallan later denied making the appointment to UCC.

There was always some sort of trouble in Philadelphia right through. That was one of the conflicts between John Panchuk and Gallan, which was rooted in the fact that there had been two refugee relief committees set up in the United States, which only later came together. Old tensions still existed, much as they did in UCC, and these were only settled after it was agreed that John Panchuk would be president of the new United Ukrainian American Relief Committee and Gallan its executive director, in charge of day-to-day operations.

Walter Gallan was a post-World War One veteran. He was a nationalist, his heart was in Lviv and so on. Panchuk was Canadian born, but a naturalized American citizen since childhood, by adoption. Possibly he was more American than Ukrainian, or maybe equally, but certainly he was not as rabid a nationalist as Gallan, who may have been OUN Solidarists oriented. So while John Panchuk's approach to all problems was like ours, totally North American, Gallan's was anxiously Ukrainian nationalist. I think John Panchuk in his heart still felt all the time that Gallan was an immigrant, that this operation should be run by Americans and not by immigrants. Panchuk had excellent relations with American government circles, which was a tremendous asset to the UUARC. He was high up in the Democratic Party. He saw things our way, and later (this was after my April 1947 letter to UUARC, which so infuriated Gallan), he supported my viewpoint in many ways. Anyway, back to this question of Frolick and CURB, in October of 1946.

When we returned as a mission of which I was the head, Frolick felt (and possibly rightly so) that to join our mission as a member would be a demotion and, therefore, refused. He said he wanted to return to Canada. I felt morally indebted and obligated towards Stan since I had persuaded him to resign from CCG and join CURB. It was my feeling that if he chose not to remain we should pay his way back to Canada. He shouldn't have to suffer that expense, and he certainly didn't have the resources, I don't think. He also felt that UCC should do it. UCC eventually, I think, recognized that they should and paid his way back to Canada. And so he went, but he was bitter. Before going back to Canada, he told us, ''When I get back there I'm going to make Kushnir and all these people in UCC crawl in mud!'' In a way he kept his word. Instead of returning to UNF and its youth movement—his own parent organizations—Stan later became one of the founders of the Canadian League for the Liberation of Ukraine (LVU). This was the major post-World War Two political refugee organization in Canada. It got set up in Toronto on May 1, 1949. Before that, around mid December 1948, its adherents were already reading a new Ukrainian Canadian newspaper, *Homin Ukrainy*. Stan was its publisher. This whole organization was very much OUNr minded, or became that way soon enough.

Frolick and I were not antagonists, or at least I don't feel that way. He believed that our decision to remove him was superimposed on us by Rev. Kushnir and company in UCC. I think now that since Kushnir, president of UCC, had as his right-hand man Kossar, who was a strick *Melnykivtsi,* OUNs, that it may well have been that UCC wanted to rid itself of Frolick. But we didn't know too much about it—their inner deliberations. I certainly didn't know too much, nor did I think at that time that I was sent back to get rid of Frolick. But we soon learned all about the split in the ranks of the OUN, and this became increasingly evident in the DP camps where they had their own channels of communication and underground network. Kossar knew about the split long before I ever heard of it, or many of us, because Kossar was a strong OUN man, when it was led by Col. Konovalets and later Col. Melnyk. The OUN split later spread to Canada, after communication lines were re-established between OUN cells in Europe and Canada. I have no sure knowledge of when or how this came about, for I had no links with this movement. People like Kossar in Winnipeg, or Prof. Pavlychenko in Saskatoon, or the American Ukrainians in ODVU would know the details, not USRL members. Remember, our Orthodox movement believed in being loyal to Canada, so we refused any link to European-based organizations and took no instructions from abroad. We were independent, self-reliant, as our title suggests. Other Canadian Ukrainian organizations, like UNF, were just the opposite, they revelled in their OUN connections. Just as LVU does to this day.

One of the issues on which debate arose when we got back to England was over CURB's financial records. George Kluchevsky was CURB treasurer while we were gone and kept Frolick's books. I think they balanced. Yet Ann Crapleve, who became our treasurer at that time, checked them. We did a report together, she and I and Danylo Skoropadsky. We went through all the books. It wasn't so much that they didn't balance as that the money was used in ways that we didn't think was justified for relief work, including the publication of this Ukrainian Information Service literature and these communiqués, etc., that kind of thing. Frolick claimed that the books were in a mess when he got them, which of course was true. You see, we had three accounts: we had a CURB account, which still wasn't an incorporated body, we had our UCSA account, which we were trying to transfer from UCSA to CURB (we couldn't use the UCSA money which was solely servicemen's money for this kind of thing), and we also had a UCVA, or our veterans', account. The first $2,000 UCC sent to us (CURB) so we could operate—buy paper, hire a secretary, and such—I put into my own account, so we had three accounts. And I was paying bills which were purely CURB bills. Full records were kept, but these were confusing, fast-paced times, and that is reflected in the financial records of the period. No one misappropriated funds, ever. We all worked for the greater Ukrainian cause, although, obviously, we went our different ways when it came to deciding on the best means for doing so.

The Mission's Efforts

Anyway, Frolick went home to Canada by the end of 1946. His story thereafter he can tell you about. We were joined by Bill Byblow, a real Canadian veteran, who stayed in London and joined our mission. And so we did become five. Then from out of the blue there arrived in London Father Jean. Father Jean arrived totally on the strength of the plans and the organization of the Basilian Fathers. When he arrived in London and contacted us, we just opened our arms to him because we needed all the help we could get. He was a French Canadian, but he had taken a deep interest in Ukrainian affairs since World War One. Prior to or during that war, he had been ordained as a Greek (Ukrainian) Catholic. Originally he was a Roman Catholic. He became a Greek Catholic, I think, after Metropolitan Sheptytsky's visit to Montreal.[1] I am not

---

1. Metropolitan Andrey Sheptytsky, Prelate of the Ukrainian Catholic church in Lviv, West Ukraine, visited Canada in 1910 to firm up links with the growing Ukrainian Catholic church here.

exactly sure when. Anyway, Father Jean had become so interested that he went to Lviv and asked to be reordained in the Greek (Ukrainian) Catholic rite. And he was. He was of great help to the Ukrainians at the Brest-Litovsk negotiations and at the Paris conference negotiations after World War One because he was the only one who knew languages. He could speak French, English and Ukrainian. He became indispensable to the Ukrainian National Republic government involved in the Paris Peace Conference and in many of these affairs. Then he came back to Canada anxious to help Ukrainians. All at once in 1946 he turned up in London as a missionary. I suppose that's what he was. We joined him to us, making him the sixth member of our Canadian Relief Mission for Ukrainian Victims of War. We helped Father Jean do anything he wanted to do. While the Basilian Fathers could give him some money for the trip that was about the extent of it. So we took him in and eventually he became the founder of the Ukrainian Catholic church in England. He founded the first Ukrainian Catholic parish in London. At least he was their first pastor. In fact, if Ukrainian Catholics in Britain have anybody to be grateful to, it's Father Jean. He and I had together conducted the service at the first Ukrainian DP funeral in England for one of the EVW girls who died in Cornwall. He celebrated the Mass while I was the cantor. These were the Ukrainian DPS—titled European Voluntary Workers— whom the British were resettling in the United Kingdom, in effect making use of the DPS as a labour pool from which they could draw. Father Jean made a tremendous contribution to the resettlement and rehabilitation of both the Division and the EVWs in Britain from 1947-52 and deserves more recognition than he has received.

My wife became secretary of the mission and manager of the office in London, our headquarter's coordinator. I placed Tony Yaremovich in the British Zone in Germany, based in Lemgo. Ann Crapleve was sent in Frankfurt, that was in the American Zone (because the American Ukrainians still couldn't send anyone but were willing to fund 50 per cent of our operation until they could send one of their own people). And that's all we had. We put no one in the French Zone. Instead we shopped around for local talent. We realized that we'd have to rely on local Ukrainians, give them status and protection. So in the French Zone we found Dr. Jaroslaw Kalba, who later became executive director of UCC around 1956 after Mr. Kochan. Dr. Kalba was the man we appointed as our representative in the French Zone. The Soviet Zone we obviously couldn't touch. In London we hired Bill Byblow and Steve Yaworsky, who were assisted by Danlyo Skoropadsky and his aide, Vladimir de Korostovetz, all of them working together with AUGB, the Ukrainian Relief Committee in Manchester and newly settled Ukrainians in Britain.

Our master plan, on which we insisted and which we carried through to the end, was that each occupation zone in Germany should have its central zone committee formed from and by representatives from each Ukrainian DP camp with an umbrella committee for the whole of Austria (Central Ukrainian Relief Committee for Austria) and Germany (Central Representation of Ukrainians in Germany) coordinating all local efforts. Ukrainians in Switzerland, Italy, France, Belgium, Holland, Denmark, Finland, Norway, Sweden, Turkey, even Egypt had their own central representations or committees. We even formed a group in China (in the Harbin area) which we tried to and did help. Wasyl Mudryj became one of CURB's representatives as well, and an active one at that, in Germany. In Austria things were much simpler. Austria was reunited much sooner than Germany, so their Allied occupation zones disappeared. Austria was given its autonomy well before Germany, just after Italy. In Austria Ukrainians were united, so we didn't have to worry much about three Western zones. We didn't have anyone to spare, so they managed affairs themselves as our (CURB) representatives—the Central Ukrainian Relief Committee, in Innsbruck, Austria. They elected Dr. Myron Rosliak as their president. He eventually resettled in Edmonton about 1948-49. His secretary was another Yaroslaw Spolsky, who later resettled in Toronto. As for me, I was rather an ambassador-at-large, travelling through Europe all the time, trying to get things established and set up and trying to join the links together so that we could have an effective operation.

Since UNRRA, then the Preparatory Commission for the International Refugee Organization (PCIRO) and finally IRO were the specialized international agencies charged with caring for the DPs, I made it a special point to attend their meetings—I even submitted a memorandum on how, after July 1, 1947, IRO should be constituted. That was at the PCIRO meeting in Geneva. Later, we helped coordinate our CURB work with IRO, which well appreciated the work of the Voluntary Agencies Coordinating Committee in which we participated. IRO, understandably, wanted to deal with *one* Ukrainian agency and not a half dozen. I agreed and I insisted that there be as much centralization as possible, between the United Ukrainian American Relief Committee and the Ukrainian Canadian Relief Fund. In the field we could not afford to have two or three missions. We already had Father Jean overseas working almost exclusively for the Ukrainian Catholics, then there were the Protestant Evangelists (Baptist) who sent over Bishop Basil Kuziw. If there got to be too many Ukrainian relief missions in Europe, there would be repetition and wasted effort. We were already mushrooming all over the place, you see.

IRO signed contracts with each voluntary relief agency spelling out duties and responsibilities for each side since much of the financing of the agencies was done by and through IRO. Gallan outstripped us. Gallan went to this Geneva conference, signed the contract, and after that we were at their mercy. We had to get sponsorships for immigration to the United States through the UUARC, and so on. I was there all the time. In fact, they even asked me for plans, ideas and suggestions, which I gave to them through Ambassador Jean Desy, on paper as to how to set up IRO so as not to repeat the mistakes of UNRRA.

There had been a relief organization in existence prior to the formation of the UNRRA in western Europe, which was a descendent of the old, post-World War One Nansen International Office for Refugees, namely the IGCR (Inter-Governmental Committee on Refugees). These two organizations, UNRRA and IGCR, were the big authorities in all matters which concerned refugees and victims of war in Europe. Anything you wanted to do had to get their blessing. We didn't get too much from UNRRA, although what we did get was appreciated. But IGCR, possibly because it was a descendant of the Nansen group and probably because it was more British controlled, or because the people who where involved were largely ex-servicemen, was very cooperative and we had a perfect relationship with them. That relationship was kept right up until July 1947 when IRO took over refugee work. Many of the officers were ex-army and ex-air force, and we used them tremendously.

104

They helped us to emigrate thousands of people to Australia, New Zealand, places like that, because they were the ones who made the final decisions. And a lot of those people were very helpful. We moved thousands and thousands of people only by phoning someone or having a friend in the right place. W/CDR Innis was one such IGCR (later PCIRO) man.

It would take hours to detail all the good that they accomplished. But one of the things that I know of personally was with the group of Ukrainians who were stranded in Italy and who were connected with the Ukrainian Division ''Galicia.'' They were not part of it, however. They were wives, nursing sisters, families, strays who joined the retreating soldiers. There must have been a few hundred of them. And we managed to move the whole lot from Italy to England towards the end of 1947, without costing us a single penny. We had no money, only our lobbying effort and that was all. And so it was only because these people at UNRRA and IGCR believed and understood us that these Ukrainian refugees were saved. Our sympathizers spoke to the right people and saved our DPs. Many of the Division's men were reunited with their families because of this.

Another group that they helped us with was the Ukrainians who had been stranded in Liechtenstein. We moved all of these Ukrainians ouf of there without any cost to ourselves other than a few letters and phone calls—again the efficacy of our lobby could be seen at work.

Immigration and resettlement of DPs after mid 1947 was processed through and by IRO. They also helped us with repatriation. The people who were scheduled for repatriation, or who were not eligible as DPs because of old UNRRA regulations, would have been lost if our friends hadn't managed to ''legitimize'' them into refugee camps. A concrete example of this was the group of UPA soldiers who escaped in 1947 through Soviet lines to the West. At first we couldn't do anything for them, but at least gave them CARE parcels and cigarettes, which they could sell or trade on the black market for food. Eventually, they were all legitimized and put into DP camps. Most of them later emigrated. Today almost anywhere I go, I find someone who remembers me, or knows about me and our mission, from my visits to the DP camps between 1945-47.

When our year of overseas work had expired, we met in Regensburg, Germany on the occasion of a Ukrainian DP conference there, and we held a meeting of the mission. I said, "I'm going to go back to Canada. I'm going to persuade them, somehow or other, to send another team or replacement, or make some kind of a decision." There was still lots to do and the refugee problem would take much longer than a year to solve. Winnipeg asked the mission to remain a little longer and for me to come back alone and be present to help them make new arrangements. Within a very short time both Ann Crapleve and Tony Yaremovich decided on their own also to return. So the result was that three of us went back, which meant extra time, money and all of us would be off the front line. That's where we should have been, on the front lines. I was hoping that they'd stay behind, carry on. But they both decided, and I think it was Tony's influence on Ann, that they wanted to go back too. So my wife was left behind with our child to hold the fort alone. She was running the bureau with the help of Bill Byblow, Steve Yaworsky, Dr. Vladimir de Korostovetz, Danylo Skoropadsky and others left in England. We already had all these relief committees established on the Continent—Belgium, Paris, Rome with Bishop Buchko, tow or three committees in Switzerland, and so on—and they ran things on their own as usual.

Our Mission Disbands

So the three of us came back to have a meeting with UCC and UCRF. We gave a report to a mass rally (Tony Yaremovich and I both spoke), and we had many meetings with Ukrainians across Canada. At the last meeting Ann and Tony decided that they weren't going to return to England. They had their own private lives to consider and so they would stay in Canada and take care of personal interests. I wanted to do the same thing, but I couldn't. I'd left a wife and child behind in London. So I said I'd go back alone and do the best I could without anyone else for at least another year. So I went back. Within two weeks or so of my returning to London, however, both Ann and Tony turned up. I was very glad, of course, until a letter arrived from UCC telling me that the plan of operation was now different. We weren't going to be part of a single, united mission anymore, nor was there to be any centralized, London-based organization (CURB) as before. We would be reporting directly to Winnipeg and each separately. Tony and Ann were now independent field representatives for the UCRF. To me this meant that the mission was disbanded as such. Here were three, or four, separate representatives sent to Europe, and each would do work on their own. I'd work with my wife as a team, but these two would work on their own. I wouldn't necessarily know what they were doing, nor would they know what things I was up to.

The real motivation, I suspect, behind the new plan was that a few people in Winnipeg wanted total control of all European operations, believing that they could make all relevant decisions back there in Winnipeg. This, of course, was just a dream and had no practical basis—decisions had to be made quickly, on the spot, in the field, and there had to be maximum *coordination* in the field so that the left hand knew what the right hand was doing. Headquarters in Winnipeg could only give general lines of policy and guidance and provide resources and logistics.

I said to Ann and Tony, "I don't think the new structure is right. We shouldn't operate separately. What good is it? I'm going to be here in London, whatever I'm going to do. You're going to be somewhere else; you'll be sending reports to Winnipeg, Tony will be sending reports to Winnipeg. All will be sending reports to Winnipeg. They'll be getting three reports instead of one. It's bad enough now getting them to make decisions. How can we operate as a mission in the field if in fact we're going to have three missions?" So I said, "We should operate as a team, just as we did before." There was a lot to do yet. The members of the Division were still prisoners, and their future was still doubtful. So I said that if that was how the new system would be, I'd quit. So I resigned. I sent a telegram to Winnipeg and resigned as head of CURB. We separated. I only carried on for another three months as head of the mission and director of CURB. In the meantime, it was obvious that the AUGB was getting on its own feet. They had even bought a headquarters building at 49 Linden Gardens in London. Once the Division got transferred to England, the AUGB even got stronger. But they were now POWs, not SEPs, and they needed to be civilianized. I just wouldn't abandon them. Winnipeg, on the other hand, was insisting that all our efforts be directed to the Continent. I felt we could do both work in Britain and in Europe with good coordination. So Tony, Ann and I developed a fraternal agreement among ourselves. I'd concentrate on Great Britain. Ann and Tony would go to the Continent where they had been before. The only difference in the operation from before was that I was working locally and independently, no longer as a Winnipeg representative.

My Work as President of AUGB

I had been elected president of the AUGB in March 1948, so I would work with AUGB problems and do the best I could there. This was my salvation, up to a point, because I had nothing else to fall back on. The only thing that I had to tide me over personally was my war service and credits. For income my wife and I took in boarders, she did laundry. We did all kinds of things to make ends meet. We managed. I applied for my war veterans' allowance to go back to school and registered at the London University School of Slavonic and East European Studies.

In the meantime, Tony Yaremovich went to the British Zone. Ann went for a short while, one or two months, to the American Zone. By that time the UUARC had sent representatives to their zone so then she joined Tony in the British Zone. It wasn't long before Tony changed his mind again and decided to return to Canada. Ann stayed on in the British Zone as the field representative of the Ukrainian Canadian Relief Fund (UCRF), reporting directly to Winnipeg. In the American Zone the American Ukrainians took over, as well as in the French Zone and in Austria. They were quite happy. They had much more money and good contacts with the American government and officials. Roman Smook, a lawyer, was the first of the American Ukrainians that came over to represent UUARC as field representative. Their North American headquarters was in Philadelphia. Dr. Gallan kept flitting in and out. But Smook bacame the first permanent director. And after that, another lawyer (I think), Mr. Rodeck took over. They signed a contract as a voluntary agency working with IRO. We did the same with the military government in the British Zone.

108

So alone I took on the operation in England. We had in England almost a hundred camps and hostels for the DPs. They weren't camps in the same sense as prisoner-of-war camps, but they were to some extent concentrations of living quarters where the occupants were all civilians. There were two categories of workers: EVWs, who had come as immigrants under the control of the British Ministry of Labour, and there were the civilianized Division veterans, controlled jointly by the British War and Home Offices. They were all equal. But in 75 per cent of the camps usually a handful of *Banderivtsi,* but sometimes *Melnykivtsi* would take over, you see. They'd seize internal control of these places and make them centres of political propaganda work, trying to sway other DPs over to their political positions and worldview. Most of the immigrants were just people who wanted jobs and to resettle and start raising a family. They weren't political, nor did most of them really expect ever to get back to Ukraine. The political refugees of the OUNr type were opposed to that kind of thinking. They wanted to mobilize everyone in support of OUN-UHVR-UPA—hopefully to somehow force their way back to their homeland. They had a compulsive need to return home—or to their conception of the place they had been forced to leave. It was their psychological condition, which they translated into political action.

There were two main operations. One was the civilianization of these 8,000 Division ex-SEPs, now POWs. And then, by that time, all the western countries had agreed that they wanted some of this labour to help in the reconstruction of their war-ravaged countries. So there was a great movement to get rid of the war victims, DPs, refugees and the like from Germany and Austria, through various plans (i.e., "Westward Ho") to anywhere they could be fruitfully employed. France, Holland, Belgium and Great Britain all took a lot of people. Great Britain took about 20,000 of these EVWs. They were brought in under contract to the Ministry of Labour to do ordinary work in agriculture, the textile industry, mines and factories. There wasn't too much difference between their status as EVWs and as inmates of the German labour system except that this was under democratic labour conditions—differences in philosophy, but not too much in methodology. The AUGB published brochures and pamphlets to help instruct them and organized their welfare and rehabilitation. These people didn't have homes to go to. So they were distributed all across Great Britain—YMCAS, YWCAS, Salvation Army, Ministry of Labour, Ministry of Agriculture and various organizations—all in hostels and camps. To a large extent they, in fact, replaced the German POW labour in Britain which had been used throughout the war. The labour shortage was a common problem in Europe, and it was filled by these EVWs from 1947-50.

One of the most interesting episodes in this period was an attempt in late 1948 to repatriate some of the sick and invalid POWS—medical cases of the Division like General Pavlo Krat—to Germany. The Division, I've said, had been brought in from Italy as a whole group in mid to late 1947. But once in the United Kingdom and redistributed among their camps and former POW camps, the British had complete control over them. I was the liaison officer with the War Office. As the AUGB we bacame, in effect, the welfare organization for all these people, and the British War Office, Home Office, Ministry of Labour, Ministry of Agriculture, Foreign Office dealt only with me as far as Ukrainians in Britain were concerned. As I've said, these workers were scattered all over. But only those who could work in the fields, plowing, milking cows, were worked. There were two categories who did not have to work extensively. One was the small group of commissioned officers. They didn't work if they didn't want to. They were all in one camp at Wolfox Lodge. They weren't a problem. They were all treated as gentlemen. The problem was with those who were not gentlemen and who were invalids—privates, a few officers too. There were about three hundred of them. And we were very worried about them. I was making practically daily visits to the War Office, trying to establish what we could do for them. They were gradually regaining their strength, taking therapy, but still there were people with TB among them, amputees, wounded, even a few with psychological problems.

Somebody, who I'm not sure, although I suspect it was in the Home Office and came from people who were certainly not our friends, had persuaded the British Cabinet and Prime Minister Atlee that England was not responsible for these people. They had never done anything for England and were a burden, so they should be dumped back onto the German economy. After all, this source argued, these Ukrainians had worn German uniforms, so why not let the Germans now be responsible for them? The decision was made during Christmas break when the House of Commons was not sitting. This happened totally without my knowledge even though I thought I had this good link with the War Office. I remember that, at that time, my office was at 64 Ridgemount Gardens, near the British Museum. I was still the president of the AUGB, and we got a message from the invalids and sick saying that they were being shipped off to Germany on the following Friday, only three days away. It was December 26, 1948, just after we had all listened to the Queen's Christmas Message of "Greetings to the Empire."

This was a great shock. I called an emergency meeting at the AUGB office now at 49 Linden Gardens. We decided to call out a general strike of all the Ukrainians. We would count on the loyalty and discipline of our own people—the POWs, the EVWs and the civilians. We believed they would listen to us. So I typed up a special petition and I got the head of the Ukrainian Catholic mission in Great Britain at that time, Father Jean, and Father Hubarshewsky, the head of the Orthodox one (sent there by Metropolitan Polikarp) to sign it also. In this appeal from the three of us, led by me as head of the AUGB, we asked our people not to go to work on the following day. Instead we instructed them to call meetings of our people, explain to them how the invalids were being shipped out to be dumped on the German economy without our knowledge or consent and that we were prepared to look after them. We asked people to go out on strike to demonstrate that we were concerned about the fate of our kin.

We sent this petition out to every Ukrainian camp in Britain, asking that they all be signed and sent to Prime Minister Atlee. Thank God, I didn't know how, but it worked. Nearly thirty thousand people around Great Britain refused to go to work. I don't know if there were any exceptions. At the same time I wrote a letter to the Queen and said that I had heard the royal message, but that our Christmas was now spoiled by Her Majesty's Government's decision to ship these unfortunates off to Germany. I told her that our Ukrainian Christmas was still two weeks off and asked her what kind of Christmas they would have in Germany, three hundred sick people being shipped off to an alien foreign land for "their" Christmas. I sent this letter to the British press and publicized our grievance as much as possible. And we called on every friend we had—the Archbishop of Canterbury, prelates in the Roman Catholic and Anglican churches, all of our friends in Parliament like Mr. Richard Stokes, Tracy Philipps (who wrote letters to the editor of the *London Times*) and many others. We mobilized everybody that we knew who could possibly help. Most added their concern to our chorus of protest. And the British press picked it up. Several hundred articles and columns were given over to carrying the news of the "general strike of Ukrainian voluntary workers in Britain."

This all happened during Parliament's Christmas break. It must have struck home because somebody in the Cabinet (I don't know who) decided that the decision was to be reversed. And it was. They cancelled the deportation except for two small categories of men, overall only a very small group. One category was composed of thirty to forty people who wanted to go back to Germany of their own free will, since they knew of family or relatives who now lived among the refugees. They wanted to get out of the POW camps in Britain and be reunited with their families. And there were thirty to forty additional people whose past conduct (I've never followed this up) made them supposedly "bad" guys, POWs who had really done something wrong and were being punished by being sent back to Germany. Something had happened to convince the authorities that these were undesirables as far as Great Britain was concerned. So these men were chained and shackled and sent back under escort with the volunteer repatriates. Some seventy-nine men in total were shipped back to Germany. We didn't raise too much of an issue about that since we were so happy to have saved the remaining 250 or so. We accepted that as it was. I wrote a letter to all of those who had helped us, thanking them for helping and ensuring that these sick Ukrainians could now enjoy their own Christmas in the United Kingdom, and we undertook to look after them collectively.

All of these "strikers" volunteered to tax themselves one shilling per pay cheque to create a mutual aid fund. With that money we bought a farm outside London and set up a hospital. We then took over caring for these people with the British authorities providing only specialized medical and required hospital treatment. Otherwise, we took over complete responsibility. That

AUGB Invalids Farm still exists. Many of the people recovered completely and went on to be productive citizens. That was one of the biggest highlights of our United Kingdom efforts. It was unexpected, but one of those many moments when I stuck out my neck without second thoughts only because I believed it had to be done.

CURB Is Liquidated: a New Phase in Canadian Ukrainian Relief Operations

From that period on, it was on December 11, 1948 that Ann and Tony wrapped up CURB. I had a hand in dissolving CURB also, at UCC's request. Ann Crapleve, Danylo Skoropadsky and I closed it down. We sold the furniture. We gave the library to AUGB, and we shipped some of the stuff to Winnipeg. There was a little problem over AUGB and CURB finances, but it was straightened out. Anyway we wrapped up everything and CURB ceased to exist. Tony got homesick; he had had enough. It was getting too big for him alone. He had been CURB director just prior to this, from when I resigned to the liquidation. Before when we were each part of a mission, we all mutually supported each other. One could reap the harvest of other people's contribution and so on. But now we were each separate and alone. That made it tougher on the individual. Anyway, he decided he was going back home. So he gave UCC notice, packed up and left. Ann Crapleve was the only one left in the British Zone. She became the UCRF's director in Europe.

Mr. and Mrs. Stan Wasylyshen came over from Winnipeg as representatives of the Ukrainian Canadian Relief Fund in March 1949, and Mr. Wasylyshen became director of UCRF in Europe assisted by his wife and Crapleve. He was a post World War One immigrant, a military man. Mrs. Anne Wasylyshen was Canadian born, I think. In the interwar period he worked for Cunard Steamships for ten to fifteen years and so knew something of immigration procedures. And he wanted a year in Europe. He was to a certain extent a godsend to UCC. He certainly pleased Rev. Kushnir and Kossar because he was an ardent OUNs man. He would, therefore, be dependable enough to prevent the UCRF from falling into the hands of any OUNr members. My wife and I made them feel at home in England, introduced them around, just before they went to the Continent. They spent about a year in the British Zone. He was senior field director at Lemgo with Ann Crapleve as his deputy. Later they switched operations to Bielefeld. We cooperated closely. After a short stretch the Wasylyshens also returned to Canada in 1950, and Ann Crapleve remained in charge alone until 1952. We eventually formed a central committee of all those relief organizations and committees in 1949 called the Co-ordinating Committee of Central Ukrainian Voluntary Organizations in Western Europe. We had a number of conferences in London, Paris and so on. It still exists and is now part of the World Congress of Free Ukrainians. And we gradually passed on the entire load of work and responsibility for Ukrainian war victims onto the local population in each country. This continued until 1952 when, although I was still deeply involved, I was no longer indispensable. These people whom we had shepherded for the first few years after World War Two could now take care of themselves. Or so they said. I had some doubts, primarily because of the vicious political squabbling that seemed to become ever more characteristic of the Ukrainian DPs as time went on, from 1945. For example, by mid March 1949, two organizations had emerged in the United Kingdom—the AUGB and the Federation of Ukrainians in Great Britain (FUGB). Why had this occurred? It's a good example of why I grew disillusioned to some extent with these political emigrés' politics. I remember one letter I sent in early 1949 to the British Ministry of Labour where I summed up my feelings about this factional politics in the diaspora:

> ALL refugees and DP's, whatever their nationality, consider themselves POLITICAL REFUGEES (although many of them are far from that) and therefore feel that their prime and most important duty and mission as 'emigrés' is to carry on political work and activities, for the liberation of, and their own ultimate return to, their native land... The MAJORITY, however, are really and in actual fact ECONOMIC REFUGEES as most people who have had to deal with them.... have learned, as I did. Most of them have always been in search of a place to live where they will be better off....
>
> The so-called 'politicial refugees' have often and at every opportunity IMPOSED and forced their influence on the economic refugees, and the real and actual WAR VICTIMS, and thus 'coloured' all refugees and DP's....
>
> The hardest problem that we had to solve, was HOW TO ELIMINATE POLITICS from relief and welfare work....

Internal Struggles in AUGB

Anyway, the split came about while I was president of the AUGB. In England I suppose it started with the Ukrainian Youth Association (SUM). SUM was revived in the DP camps of Germany where they set up branches in every camp. It was totally an OUNr group. Their only competition at that time was Plast, a boy scout organization which tended to have an OUNs tinge to it. But we didn't see any future for either one in the United Kingdom. Here, we felt, was new terrain and it was settled by new people. The best thing to do was to start from scratch. Don't try to transfer or transplant European organizations from the DP camps in Germany or from western Ukraine to Great Britain. This was my feeling. I said that we should have an organization of youth within the AUGB. I felt that the young people should be organized, like CUYA in Canada. We didn't have to follow any pattern and we didn't have to transplant anything.

When the OUNr's hierarchy formed SUM and presented the AUGB with a *fait accompli*—"here we are and we're organized and we demand certain powers and rights"—my attitude was opposed to them, I didn't appreciate their mode of working, nor did I feel this was the way we should do it. It should start the other way around. We would establish the pattern of how to organize our youth, our women and our schools. They could integrate into that. That was the beginning of the trouble.

The other thing that was transplanted from Europe to us in Great Britain and which was unnecessary was the split between OUNr and OUNs. When we had organized the AUGB we didn't ask which political group a person belonged to, as long as they were Ukrainian and in Great Britain they were eligible. That was it. But each group was still competing for power—who would be head of a camp committee, camp police, local schools, welfare committees—who would, in effect, control the emigration. This struggle spread in tandem with the resettlement from the DP camps of these people to Holland, Belgium, France, Italy and eventually, with further resettlement, into Canada, the United States, Great Britain, Argentina, Brazil, Australia, New Zealand, wherever DPs eventually or finally settled.

There were other political intrigues as well. I was not aware of all of them as fully, but I never thought they would have any

115

serious influence in the AUGB because I was certain that we were too well established and united. I was wrong. The *Hetmantsi* had their own group, and one of them was very active on the AUGB board of directors and with whom I was quite friendly, even back to UCSA days—Danlyo Skoropadsky. In 1948 there was a Ukrainian National Rada (Ukrainian National Council) formed in Regensburg, Germany with the help of Dr. Kushnir. The president was Andrij Livytskyj. We were involved as consultants. UNRada was supposed to be a central representative council of all the Ukrainian factions abroad—the continuation of the Ukrainian government-in-exile which went to Warsaw in the interwar period. But we were not aware of the fact that there was a power struggle going on in this Ukrainian National Council, that sides were being taken.

On one side were the OUNS with the socialists. On the other side were the OUNr and the *Hetmantsi*. The *Hetmantsi* didn't take a real leadership role because they said—and I don't buy this—that the Council accepted the platform of the last government of the Ukrainian National Republic that went into exile in Poland—the Petliura government. Of course, they considered themselves to be the heirs to governmental legitimacy, for they were supporters of Hetman Skoropadsky's regime, which the Petliura government had ousted.[1] So they refused to sit on the Council—feeling that to do so would involve having to recognize Petliura's Directorate as valid—which they obviously could not do without betraying their own monarchist background. The *Hetmantsi* (followers of Hetman Pavlo Skoropadsky and, after his death in 1945, his son Danylo Skoropadsky) never joined the Ukrainian National Council. Anyway, by 1950, the *Banderivtsi* withdrew from the Council, claiming that their ties with the UHVR and the short-lived government of June 30, 1941 (Lviv) of which Yaroslav Stetsko had been premier, has the only legitimacy they needed. So why should they belong to a World War One period government-in-exile?

---

1. Symon Petliura (born May 10, 1879) was a Ukrainian political and military leader during the liberation struggles of 1917-21, and head of the Directorate, which held power in Ukraine during 1919. He was assassinated in Paris May 25, 1926 by a Bolshevik agent.

So all this politics was transplanted. As it happened, at the second annual meeting of the AUGB in March 1949—about which we were very confident for everything had been going nicely up to then and we had no worries—all at once, after the reports were heard, a fellow stood up in the audience and says, "I move a vote of confidence to everybody *except* the president, Mr. Panchuk. For him *no* vote of confidence!" And then they started howling and whistling. And before we knew it the meeting was all in chaos. This was so well engineered, so well timed—the OUNr had people at the various spots around the hall. The cat calls, the clapping, the boos, the cheers, all of it came at the right time. When we saw what was happening, I got up and made my farewell speech. I said that I'd come there as a volunteer from Canada to help. If, in these circumstances and in this community, my help was no longer required, well goodbye. And I walked out. A sizeable group of the people in the audience walked out with me, mostly OUNs supporters and East and mainly Orthodox Ukrainians. I didn't instigate or plan that. I really wasn't interested.

So it turned, without any need for it, into an East Ukrainian-West Ukrainian/Orthodox-Catholic split—an OUNs-OUNr split. The OUNs people called a meeting right there and then at 49 Linden Gardens and formed a Federation of Ukrainians in Great Britain (FUGB). Vyacheslav Kochanivsky became president of the Federation. I wasn't interested. I just wasn't interested in Britain anymore. I was hoping soon to get back to Canada. I wasn't interested in European politics to the extent that I would lead a faction or do anything like that at all. Kochanivsky was their president for a few years, an ardent OUNs. The federation still exists today, and although it is not as big or strong as AUGB, which had a head start and a captive membership, they are there to stay. The incumbent president is Andrij Kostiuk.

I wrote a number of letters to various Ukrainians to let them know what happened in the AUGB. Let me read parts of a few for you. On March 15 I sent a letter to Ann Crapleve, and this is what I recorded about the *coup d'etat* in our British organization:

The *Hetmantsi* (Skoropadsky and CO.) have formed a very strong block with the OUN(r)—the *Banderivtsi,* the reason being their mutual agreed opposition to the Ukrainian National Council. This, of course, was the root and basis of the entire matter. They resorted

117

further to every method, legal and illegal, under the sun in which to assure that they should control and arranged to have present at the meeting a large number of guests and visitors who, although not authorized delegates, supported them very vociferously both in speech, by hand-clapping, by hooting, howling... at the right moment and at a general signal. This, of course, created a stampede in the true meaning of the word (as understood in Calgary) and the final result was that all the 'solid' and dependable people who could not agree with such methods... walked out... and left them to finish....

Most of the attacks were directed against my own person since they feared above all else the fact that I might return to power and thus continue to guarantee the Ukrainian National Council... moral and material aid and support from the AUGB. The new Council, if we agree to recognize them (which the majority are still reluctant to do...) consists of Skoropadsky–Honourary President, Dr. O. Fundak–President, O. Moncibovych–Vice-President, T. Danyliw–Secretary, and then followed by Sylenko, Dolynehyj, Korostovetz and a few more very doubtful and suspicious types, some of whom are regular visitors to the Soviet Embassy.

I would say, looking back on all of this, that there were several characteristics that typified those who forced me out of the AUGB. The people who did so were those who were against the Ukrainian National Council (UNRada), who had a personal dislike for me, who supported Catholics against Orthodox Ukrainians (or vice versa), who were inspired by communist or other foreign agents, and, perhaps most importantly, were people devoted to the cause of keeping Ukrainians separated and disorganized so as to make them weak, while creating suspicion among the British people with regard to the quality of these newly arriving immigrants in Britain. Those hotheads, as I wrote back to Canada, essentially felt that I was pro-British and not, in their terms, what they'd call "a real Ukrainian."

I suppose it all was inevitable. All because the beat, the measure, the policies, the decisions were all established somewhere outside the United Kingdom. The OUNr were convinced that there was going to be another conflict, another world war, that this whole stay overseas in western Europe, even in England, was temporary and that whatever existed abroad had to be under their control because they would use that as a base from which to go back to Ukraine. Which really wasn't at all realistic. So their aim was to take over control. And they did take over control. In Belgium, three months or so after our meeting in London, the same thing happened. Mr. Hrab and Mr. Kishka were declared *persona non grata* even though they had done so very very much to put their relief committee on its feet, established a base, scholarships, sent fifteen or twenty students to university, done much good work. They were more or less booted out. The OUNr also took over control in France. They eventually pretty well took over control in Germany. Right now they control most of those points. And they almost took over the whole of the Division. Likely not a coincidence that by May 1949 they felt secure enough to set up their LVU here in Canada. All a very well thought out plan.

It had started in the camps really. That's where you had a captive audience—human beings were easy victims to mass behaviour in the camps. Let me give you an example. In 1947-48 the Division was totally pro-Panchuk. If you'd found one person who criticized me, the majority would have lynched him. But by 1949, well, one-third of them were questioning me. What did I get out of helping them get to the United Kingdom? A pay-off perhaps for making them the slave labourers of the British, still in camps only now in the United Kingdom. I don't feel that I was betrayed by the DPs as a whole, only by a small group of people, all of whom I could almost name. In the Division Dliaboha, now deceased, was the ring leader behind that whole stampede meeting of March 1949. Even now the OUNr in the United Kingdom still won't recognize that I was once president of AUGB. It's as if I never existed for them. I feel disappointed that we spent so much time and energy on things that we needn't have worried about, instead of accomplishing so much more that we could have.

Aftermath: New Ukrainian Organizations Emerge

As soon as this split occurred, I resigned the presidency of AUGB and informed Winnipeg. So did the Wasylyshens, who had just then in March 1949 come to Britain. UCC felt that they still must have someone overseas, so they decided to open a separate office. "We can find money, we'll give you a small budget, we don't expect you to do big things, we don't want you to travel because we don't have that kind of money. But we want our own office to be separate from either AUGB or the federation, or any of the political immigration movement. We want our Canadian work to be separate, but write a personal private letter to Kushnir." He would bring it up at the meeting as his idea. So Volodymyr Kochan (then executive director of UCC—a former *Sejm* representative and member of the Ukrainian National Democratic Alliance party, later the Front for National Unity, in West Ukraine—and anti-OUN) wrote to me, I wrote to Kusnir, Kushnir came to the UCC meeting and said, "We should do this, we should do that."

The purpose of having a UCC representative over there was for lobbying. To help our mission in the field place the refugees. We lobbied every embassy, e.g., Venezuela, Columbia, Argentina, Brazil, Australia, and spoke to anyone who would listen. I had one secretary there, Mrs. Luigis, and we operated from 64 Ridgemount Gardens, near the British Museum and London University. It became the Ukrainian Bureau, European Office of UCC, and I was again in charge. It carried on, cooperating with anyone who came and asked for help because I was still the only one who had the inside track on immigration, starting with Canada and all the other embassies. I never denied the AUGB any cooperation, but, nevertheless, they were very anxious about what I might be doing. They tried to take it over. Dr. Fundak, who succeeded me as president of AUGB and Teodor Danyliw, the first and for a number of years continuous secretary of AUGB, both tried hard. Danylo Skoropadsky also remained in the AUGB, he agreed to be re-elected and became a member of their new board of directors. These three were all used, they later all left the AUGB, bitter at how the OUNr's cadres outmanoeuvred them in the AUGB.

So from 1950-52 Ukrainian Canadians had two European representations—Ann Crapleve was the field representative of the Ukrainian Canadian Relief Fund on the Continent in the British Zone of Germany at Bielefeld, attending solely to relief, welfare and resettlement for DPs; and the Ukrainian Canadian Committee (UCC) European bureau in London, headed by myself and concerned with matters of a more political nature, an office of general information and with special interest in the Division now civilianized in Britain. In the American Zone Dr. Smook and later Mr.

120

Rodeck headed the United Ukrainian American Relief Committee operations, and we cooperated as much as we could until 1952, when Ann decided she had no reason to continue on in Germany. She had married a British army captain (Smith), and she wanted to return to Canada.

By 1952 all that was left in Europe of refugees and displaced persons was the residue—the so-called "hard core." Their ultimate disposal was problematic. Some would be integrated into the German economy, some were medical cases waiting for further treatment, some were large families with elderly or very small dependants whose resettlement would take time. For us to remain much longer would be a dedication for a longer period of time. My wife and I had two children already, and there wasn't much left to do. It was routine social welfare work, for which one had to be prepared to stay five to ten years. The peak of the immigration had already finished. But what really persuaded me to return to Canada was a telegram that I got from Ambassador Jean Desy, who was in Ottawa. He was our Canadian Ambassador in Brazil during World War Two. When the war ended and Italy was liberated, Ambassador Jean Desy was transferred to Rome. He also became our Canadian representative to PCIRO and later to IRO. We had become good friends since 1946, and I had helped him with his work at PCIRO sessions. The Canadian government decided to bring him back (sometime in 1951, I believe) and make him director general of the International Service at the Canadian Broadcasting Corporation (CBC). Prior to that in London, we had been badgering the British Broadcasting Corporation (BBC) and the various western governments to do more broadcasting in the Ukrainian language. UCC had carried on a similar campaign for Ukrainian broadcasting on the CBC, with various memoranda and delegations to the government in Ottawa. When External Affairs decided that a Ukrainian Section would be opened at the CBC, they were shopping around for someone.

Ambassador Desy contacted me about whether I would be interested in coming back to Canada to set up the Ukrainian Section of the International Service at the CBC. I replied that of course I would. Lester B. Pearson was the Minister for External Affairs at the time, and he was using John Decore, MP, as his consultant in search of a suitable candidate in the Ukrainian community to set up and head the Ukrainian Section. When Desy mentioned me to Decore, he (Decore) jumped at the suggestion. Together they went to Pearson and I got a telegram as a result to "come at once." I did. I left my wife and children to do the packing and follow me later.

I took the first plane out of London for Montreal. I had an interview and started working the next day as head of the Ukrainian Section. My wife and children joined me by boat. That's how and why we ended up in Montreal. We informed UCC that we'd pulled out of Europe. Pulled a UCC on them, treating them just as they had us when we'd been involved in refugee relief operations. Even so, I later felt somewhat guilty because I walked out on UCC. I suppose eventually everyone turns into "a rat." And I "ratted" only because I really was tired and had enough.

Ukrainian DPs in Canada: Their Input

New blood—what we all hoped would enliven Canadian Ukrainian life—did not come into our already established Ukrainian Canadian organizations. Yet we needed that new blood, people who spoke better Ukrainian than we did, people who could give us new information. Instead of that, new organizations were formed and splits within the old ones. Even now they still think as if they are "they," and we are "we," and east is east and west is west, and that these second- and third-generation Canadians are not the same sort of people as the newcomers feel themselves to be. They have the attitude that "We are from the real soil, we are pure blood Ukrainians"—and they make you feel bad, lesser than them. We heard about the Canadian League for the Liberation of Ukraine (LVU) being formed on May 1, 1949. I was negatively inclined towards it, not because it was pro-OUNr, but because it was unnecessary. I couldn't have cared less who organized it. My conviction was, and still is, that there was no need for new organizations for Ukrainians in Canada after World War Two. We had everything that we possibly needed here. A pattern of Ukrainian organizations had developed from the original pioneers, there were religious and secular organizations. All sorts of organizations existed before World War Two—the majority had sorted themselves out. You had Ukrainian Catholic, Orthodox, communists, the nothings, the nationalists around UNF and the small *Hetmantsi* (UHO)

122

group. We'd sorted ourselves out for good or bad, for better or for worse. Organizations should be formed only according to need. Many of the new organizations (post World War Two) were duplications of what we already had. They were superfluous, so we thought. Of course, the political refugees, the militants, thought differently.

So when I visited the different camps in Europe in 1945, 1946 and later, I told them at the meetings they always called and asked me to address that we had all the bases they could possibly need already in Europe. But they insisted that they were a "political emigration" with very clear aims, like the liberation of Ukraine. What could they do, they asked me, if and when they got to Canada? And I told them over and over again, "If you come to Canada or the United States, or Australia, New Zealand or Great Britain, you have new ground and you've got to start from scratch. In France, Belgium and the like, there are some older people, although weakening—but in North America we have pretty well established every organization that we require for our needs. If you feel in your hearts that you are primarily interested in promoting the Catholic church, then you have that Ukrainian church there and its affiliated organizations to support. If you're more interested in secular matters, there's the UCC. For the nationalists, there was UNF. For Orthodox DPS, the USRL and CUYA." The field was there, the same as on the Orthodox side. "Just spread your wings," I said to them, "and as long as you have the time, energy, desire and money, you can do anything. The sky's the limit." We just needed new blood and more hands to work. I told them to join what already existed and serve the Ukrainian national cause, united. Many took my advice and have greatly enriched our existing Ukrainian Canadian fabric. Most went off to join their own newcomers' groups. We were all of us Canadian Ukrainians, gravely disappointed to see this happen.

Many DPS didn't agree with my views. When they came here they founded new organizations, unnecessary ones. LVU is one of them. SUZERO is another. SUM and ODUM were equally unnecessary when CUYA, YUN and UCYO already existed. But UNF was eventually taken over, however, by OUNS cadres. If Kossar had been a little more broadminded—he had tremendous influence—he might have brought all Ukrainian nationalists into UNF and dealt with

123

their internal problems there. Instead, he made his decision, a priori, even before they started coming, that UNF was to be OUNs, that the rest were rebels, dissidents, people who were "enemies." So the OUNr had little alternative but to form a new organization. They could have tried to go into UNF—a few at first did—and tried to work inside it. Most didn't. Six of one, half dozen of another, if "fault" is to be assigned. The refugees (DPs) could have settled into our organization. They *could* have. It was a question of good-will and adaptation—a logical approach. Some fault for the disruptive outcome rests on both sides.

At a funeral I attended recently in Lachine, Quebec, there was a great steel fence in the cemetery, eight feet high, dividing the cemetery of the old-time Ukrainians from that of the newcomers. There's no difference between the people, but they're buried on different sides of the fence—an iron curtain between the dead. What have we learned when you see that sort of barrier? It's all a problem of education, as once there was a problem of education between those who called themselves Ruthenians and the nationally conscious people who titled themselves Ukrainians. The DPs could have merged with the old emigration in Canada. Today in Lachine the majority of the graves are on the old side—an interesting symbol. It's only in eastern Canada that you really see this stand out so glaringly. In western Canada you don't see it. Most DPs settled in eastern urban areas. The DPs in western Canada were a minority who fell easily into place, into established patterns. In the east, where they came in clusters, bigger groups, they kept separate. "Why be swallowed by somebody else?" they said. "It's better to be a big fish in a small pond than a sardine in an ocean."

So they took over or built new groups, for example, in Toronto at 404 Bathurst Street where the Orthodox church came to be dominated by newcomers. We once had a CUYA there of two hundred members. In 1940 when I was going overseas they gave me a big farewell. They have a history behind them. Today, it's a totally, totally new Canadian cathedral—no CUYA, only ODUM. Not much linking the pre-World War Two people to the new ones except the building. They took over the cathedral. Why? For its identity. But that identity could have been preserved, continuity kept, if there had been more of a "joining together." Unfortu-

124

nately, we pre-World War Two Canadian Ukrainians couldn't on our own produce enough priests. So we imported these DP priests. But all of them—of the new immigration—had very little in common with us. So in St. Vladimir's Cathedral in Toronto you have Rev. Foty, a newcomer, who followed Rev. Sametz, a pioneer. What happened? The people who were there before left St. Vlad's and went to other Orthodox parishes—Long Branch or Scarborough—to be with their own and abandoned St. Vladimir's. Five miles to St. Vlad's is equal to five miles travelling into Scarborough. So the old-timers abandoned their church, pulled out. And now the cathedral is almost totally a DP church. Of course, there's a different evolution for the Ukrainian Catholics. Most of the Catholics were West Ukrainians, whereas the Orthodox were psychologically atomized, products of over twenty years of Soviet rule. East Ukrainians of the postwar vintage are suspicious people. It's a different mentality. For the Ukrainian Catholics it was easier to find common ground. The barrier was really between East and West Ukrainians, Orthodox and Catholic believers, the OUN of the west, the individualism of the east.

Thinking Back

I spent a total of eleven years overseas. What did it cost me personally? I ended up flat broke and had to worry about my finances and building my own life anew in Canada. My continual commitment has cost me materially, for I never charged a price for my labour or asked for a salary while we were overseas serving the Ukrainian cause. Others became very rich. But who, at that time, knew I'd be gone as long as I was? When I made the deal in Winnipeg, I thought I'd be gone for only one year. I'm a good touch, I guess. Nobody planned. In hindsight now, I don't know if I should have done it. By nature I think I would have. But I would never have married then or had children. I would have tried to make it on my own. Once I married and we reached the stage of having a family, it was not fair to so impose on my family. I owed them a better life. But the cause was there to be served—there was the principle of saving our fellow Ukrainians at stake. That had been my father's commitment—serving Ukraine—it was innate in me. Happily, I served, and my wife and children stayed beside me. I'm thankful. For me it is a matter of calling, of feel-

125

ing. It is not tangible. You can't even pin it down. I was fortunate, however, in having an understanding wife who felt much as I did and went along with me.

I wasn't properly rewarded for my services by the Ukrainians in Canada—barely remembered—but I don't care. I'm rewarded by God and my conscience. If I had to do the same thing over again, I suppose I would and I wouldn't regret making such a choice, nor would I worry about the consequences. I never had an ulterior motive, never. I never even wanted to be a commissioned officer except for UCSA's sake. I gave, or tried to, all of myself to them as my mother had done for me with her tremendous self-sacrifice. I felt that here were people in need and I should do something for them. When I was in CUYA, teaching Ukrainian school in the RCAF and UCSA, I saw lots of Ukrainian work that needed doing, many desperate souls lying around who had to be picked up, brushed off and set back to work, helping themselves. I committed myself and I've kept up. The war created an opportunity that you couldn't have created yourself for begging, and we grabbed it! I did what I could, as well as I could and never for one moment was there any thought of personal reward or recognition. There was only the satisfaction of doing something which needed doing badly. I'm thankful to have served.

Chronology of Events

1914
Feb. 8   Gordon Bohdan Panchuk born on a homestead near Peterson, Saskatchewan

1935
June   Panchuk completes Saskatoon Normal School and begins teaching in Yellow Creek, Saskatchewan

1939
Sept. 1   World War Two begins; shortly after, Panchuk enrolls at the University of Saskatoon where he also joins the COTC

1940
Nov. 7-9   UCC is formed in Winnipeg
1940-41   Panchuk transfers to the RCAF and is moved first to the Manning Depot in Toronto and later to No. 1 RCAF Wireless School in Montreal

1941
December   Panchuk is posted overseas to Bournemouth, England from where he is sent to Ulster, Northern Ireland

1943
Jan. 7   First Get-Together for Ukrainian Canadian servicemen and the Manchester Ukrainian community held at the Ukrainian Social Club in Manchester; UCSA is formed; the president is Bohdan Panchuk
Jan. 31   Panchuk elected president of the Ukrainian Social Club in Manchester; Mr. J. Lesniowsky is secretary
May 2   Second Get-Together to celebrate Ukrainian Easter and Mother's Day; Rhys Davies, MP, is one of the special guests present
June 22-24   First UCC Congress held in Winnipeg
July 31-Aug. 1   Third Get-Together—the first to take place in Lon-

	don—held at the Canadian Legion building
August	UCSA selects the Vicarage building at 218 Sussex Gardens, Paddington, where the Services Club is established
September	First issue of the *UCSA Newsletter* distributed
Nov. 3	Corporal Panchuk becomes Pilot Officer Panchuk

1944

Jan. 6-7	Fourth Get-Together of UCSA to celebrate Ukrainian Christmas and first anniversary of the organization; P/O Panchuk re-elected president
Apr. 13-16	Official opening of UCSA Services Club in London (the fifth Get-Together)
Summer	Rev. S. Sawchuk (Ukrainian Orthodox) and Rev. M. Horoshko (Ukrainian Catholic) arrive in England
June 6	D-Day—Ukrainian Canadian servicemen begin encountering Ukrainian DPs; John Karasevich and Bohdan Panchuk mentioned in the military despatches
Nov. 25-26	First UCSA Get-Together in Brussels with Rev. Hermaniuk celebrating the Divine Liturgy; Mykola Hrab appointed by CURB to head a Ukrainian relief committee in Belgium—the first group of this kind

1945

Jan. 6-7	Sixth Get-Together and second UCSA anniversary; a Rome Get-Together held by Central Mediterranean Theatre troops with Bishop I. Buchko officiating
Jan. 18	UCRF authorized by the Canadian government
Feb. 18	Panchuk reprimanded by UCSA executive in London for his activities on behalf of the Ukrainian DPs; he resigns in protest (not accepted); he remains president of UCSA and active in refugee relief work
May	Stanley W. Frolick in Britain with CCG
May 5	Seventh UCSA Get-Together—a joint celebration of Ukrainian Easter and Mother's Day; Manchester Ukrainian mothers are especially honoured
May 8	V-E Day
June 21	On the advice of M. Hrab, Dmytro Andrievsky, appointed to compile information on Ukrainian DPs in the American and British Zones of Germany, estimated some 4.5 million Ukrainian DPs were there
June 27	Memorandum presented to SHAEF arguing that Ukrain-

	ian DPs should be segregated from Poles and Russians, that Ukrainian-language radio broadcasts should be produced and that Ukrainian-language newspapers should be distributed; requested clarification of repatriation question
July	Colonel A.J. Moffitt issues orders which, in part, state that neither the British nor American Military Governors of Germany recognize Ukrainian as a nationality; both prohibit the formation of any Ukrainian organizations and state that all Ukrainians will be treated according to their citizenship: as Poles, Soviets, Czechoslovaks, or "Stateless"
July-Aug.	Mass issuing of Ukrainian Red Cross identity cards to Ukrainian DPs in Unterlüss area by F/L Burianyk and F/L Panchuk
August	Association of Ukrainian Soldiers in the Polish Armed Forces created with its office at 218 Sussex Gardens
Aug. 20	Major Syrotiuk, a Military Government official stationed near Kiel, sends telegram to UCSA London, regarding the forcible repatriation from Flensburg of non-Soviet Ukrainians
Sept. 19	Operational records of CURB begin
Nov. 10-11	Tenth UCSA Get-Together in London; the official closing of the UCSA Services Club
Dec. 31	CURB officially constituted by UCC
1946	
Jan. 5-6	Rev. B. Kushnir, president of UCC and UCRF, visits London to inspect CURB and visit the DP camps; the eleventh UCSA Get-Together to celebrate Ukrainian Christmas
Jan. 19	AUGB formed
Feb. 2	Gordon R.B. Panchuk marries Anne Cherniawsky in London; shortly thereafter he returns to Germany to continue his duties with the RCAF and the British Army of Occupation on the Rhine
Feb. 7-8	Meeting of the continental Ukrainian Relief Committees at CURB headquarters in London; representatives included: Rev. Kushnir, B. Panchuk, S. Frolick, D. Andrievsky, Mr. Shumowsky and members of the Association of Ukrainian Soldiers in the Polish Armed Forces

Feb. 9	CURB staff now includes: B. Panchuk as director, S.W. Frolick as general secretary, Mrs. A. Panchuk as welfare officer and Ann Crapleve as treasurer
Mar. 25	First issue of Ukrainian Press Service appears
May 7	Mr. and Mrs. Panchuk return to Canada; S.W. Frolick becomes director of CURB, aided by George Kluchevsky, treasurer
May 29	Senate Standing Committee on Immigration and Labour holds hearings in Ottawa; debate between UCC supporters and Ukrainian communists over desirability of allowing Ukrainian DP immigration to Canada; UCC—represented by Rev. Kushnir, Rev. Sawchuk, John Solomon and B. Panchuk—is successful in its lobbying efforts
June 4-6	Second UCC Congress held in Toronto
Aug. 10	UCVA presents its Renaissance Plan to UCC
Oct. 12	CRM, later known as the Canadian Relief Mission for ·Ukrainian Victims of War, leaves for England; members include: Mr. and Mrs. Panchuk. Anthony J. Yaremovich and Ann Crapleve
Oct. 14-19	CURB again headed by Panchuk; Frolick leaves for Canada by November
Dec. 12	A. Yaremovich posted to Lemgo in the British Zone, Ann Crapleve to Frankfurt in the American Zone
Dec. 17	First memorandum about the Ukrainian Division "Galicia" issued by CURB
1947	
Jan. 25	First issue of CURB's *The Refugee* appears
Feb. 3	Panchuk participates in PCIRO meetings in Geneva
Apr. 5	The Panchuks visit Ukrainian SEP camp at Rimini
May 24	Transfer of Ukrainian SEPs to England begins; by June 6 Panchuk greets first group of them to arrive in Sheffield, England; SEP status changed to POW
July 31	CRM formally ceases to exist; its members placed on individual expense accounts
September	Bill Byblow is acting director of CURB
Sept. 11	By this date both Yaremovich and Crapleve have returned to Canada
Sept. 23	Panchuk arrives in Montreal and proceeds to Winnipeg
November	Panchuk returns to England to be director of CURB;

130

	his contractual obligation is to remain in this post until 31 April 1948
Nov. 1	Yaremovich and Crapleve sign separate agreements with UCRF to act as independent field representatives in Europe
Dec. 1	UUARC opens its Munich office with Mr. R. Smook in charge
Dec. 20	AUGB incorporated
Dec. 31	Panchuk resigns as director of CURB; Yaremovich takes over

1948
March	Panchuk becomes second president of AUGB
Aug.-Sept.	Yaremovich resigns from CURB and returns to Canada; Crapleve takes over as director of CURB
Dec. 11	On this date CURB is formally closed by a Liquidation Committee composed of Mr. Panchuk, Danylo Sko- ropadsky and Ann Crapleve (chairman)
Dec. 15	First issue of the newspaper *Homin Ukrainy* published in Toronto by S.W. Frolick
Dec. 28	Mass protest strike called out throughout Britain against the repatriation of sick and invalid Ukrainian POWs to Germany

1949
Mar. 12-13	Panchuk deposed as president of AUGB by a coalition of *Hetmantsi* and *Banderivtsi*
Mar. 15	Mr. and Mrs. E. Wasylyshen arrive in England on their way to Bielefeld where Mr. Wasylyshen becomes director of UCRF operations, aided by A. Crapleve, on April 1
Apr. 16	Formation of Ukrainian Self Reliance Groups in the U.K. and Anglo-Ukrainian Clubs in Britain by Pan- chuk; later FUGB is established to serve as an opposi- tion to AUGB
May 1	Canadian LVU is formed in Toronto; S.W. Frolick elected vice president

1950
| Feb. 7-9 | Third UCC Congress held in Winnipeg |
| Aug. 1 | UCC authorizes Panchuk to be its European represent- ative and maintain a Ukrainian Bureau in London |

Sept. 12	Mr. and Mrs. Wasylyshen return to Winnipeg; Ann Crapleve remains in Bielefeld as director of UCRF operations
Sept. 25	Members of the Ukrainian Division "Galicia" are finally granted Canadian cabinet approval to immigrate

1951
Dec. 21	Ann Crapleve leaves British Zone for England

1952
Feb. 28	Ann Crapleve leaves England for Canada
June	Panchuk leaves London to return to Canada and become head of the CBC's Ukrainian Section, International Services; conclusion of Ukrainian Canadian refugee relief and resettlement operations abroad

Appendix

BRITISH ZONE - DISPLACED PERSONS

SUBJECT: -   HQ 30 Corps District
UKRAINIANS   219/DP
                                    29 Dec. 45.

Prime Minister Attlee opening U.N.O. Conference:-

To:- Mil. Gov. Detachments - Hannover, Bassum, Celle, Oldenburg, Mappen, Brunswick, Osnabruck.

"I am glad that the Charter of the United Nations does not deal only with Governments and States or with politics and war BUT WITH THE SIMPLE ELEMENTAL NEEDS OF HUMAN BEINGS whatever be their race, their colour, or their creed. In the Charter we reaffirm our faith in fundamental human rights. We see the freedom of the individual in the State as an essential complement to the freedom of the State in the world community of nations. We stress, too, that

1. H.M.G. do not recognize Ukrainian as a nationality, and persons coming from the Ukraine are classed as citizens of the country in which they had their residence on 1 Sept, 1939. No recognition can be given to any Ukrainian Org. or rep. as such.

2. All such persons who lived in Soviet territory are compulsorily returned to the U.S.S.R. under the terms of the Yalta agreement as soon as they are proved to be such.

3. Ukrainians of other than Soviet citizenship receive education and welfare facilities in the language appropriate to their citizenship, and for the time being it is impracticable for a variety of reasons to publish books or other literature in Ukrainian.

4. All Ukrainian Organizations will be disbanded forthwith, and where they are established outside camps, the representatives will be brought into camps as normal D.P.'s. All stationery pertaining to these organizations will be confiscated.

social justice and the best possible standards of life for all are essential factors in promoting and maintaining the peace of the world.''

THE TIMES
D. Jan. 11/46.

5. Continuation of such activities is punishable under Articles 26 and/or 34 of Ordinance 1.

Brigadier,
Chief of Staff,
30 Corps District.

Ref:

U.S.A. ZONE - DI

President of the Preparatory Commission and temporary president of the General Assembly:-

"The San Francisco Charter which to-morrow we shall start to bring into effect, repeatedly stresses the vital importance of stimulating in the world real respect for fundamental liberties, individual rights, the dignity of man and the dictates of justice as an indispensable basis for the maintenance of peace and international security.''

The Times
D. Jan. 10/46

At U.N.O.
Peace Conference,
London.

C.H.P.I.D.
U.S.A.   A.P.O. 758
Military   Wiesbaden.
Government for 27th November 1945.
Gros-Hassen.

SUBJECT: Release of Soviet citizens, subject to repatriation in accordance with the Yalta agreement from labour for the Germans in the American Zone.

1. The following information is extracted from USFET letter AG388/7 GEC - AGO Subject: Release of Soviet citizens subject to repatriation, in accordance with the Yalta Agreement from labour for the Germans in the American Zone dated 7th November 1945.

2. The Senior Soviet representative for repatriation at our main Headquarters claims that the Soviet Commission on repatriation shows 18,919 persons in the Eastern Military Zone, and 2,787 persons in the Western Military Zone who he declares are Soviet citizens and subject to repatriation in accordance with the Yalta agreement.

He claims further that these persons are working in German factories and on farms. He has

134

formally demanded that our main Headquarters should forbid the German employers from employing Soviet citizens.

3. You are requested to instruct the Ober-Burgrmeister or the 'Landrat' of every district that they should take the necessary steps to forbid German employers either private or public from employing any Soviet citizens who may be subject to repatriation in accordance with the Yalta agreement. These employers should be informed that only these persons who were physically present in the USSR, and who were citizens of the USSR on the 17th September 1939, and who were removed from the USSR or left the USSR beginning the 22nd June 1941, are to be considered as Soviet citizens subject to repatriation in accordance with the Yalta agreement.

4. Such Soviet citizens wil be assembled and transferred to the Camp at Noukirchen organized under Soviet administration. Similarly you will transfer from camps administered by UNRRA of Soviet citizens subject to the Yalta agreement to camps organized under Soviet administration.

It is forbidden to support this assembly and transfer by using *troops,* but no Soviet citizen subject to repatriation in accordance with the Yalta agreement will be able to benefit from assistance and support in any Displaced Persons camp after the 8th Dec/45, except those camps that are under Soviet administration.

(Sgd.) Robert Wallach, Capt.
for Lieut. Col. Newman

U.S.A. ZONE - DISPLACED PERSONS (Continued)

Prime Minister
Attlee:-

A.P.O. 758
5th Dec. 1945.

"I think, too, that at the prestime the ordinary men and women in every nation have a greater realization of what is at stake. To make this organization

U.S.A. Office of the Mil. Govt.
Stadtkreis und Landkreis Mannheim
Dt. F 16 1st Mil. Gov. Bn.

It is hereby announced that from 0800 hrs. 8th December, all foor, shelter, etc., for those Displaced Persons who have lived in the Kaiser Wilheim Caserne, and who in accordance

135

a living reality we must enlist the support not only of Governments, but of the masses of the people throughout the world. They must understand that we are building a defence for the common people..
.. Every individual can be brought to realize that the things that are discussed in conference here are the concern of all and affect the home life of every man, woman, and child. Without social justice and security there is no real foundation for peace, for it is among the socially disinherited and those who have nothing to lose that the gangster and aggressor recruit their supporters.''

The Times,
D. Jan. 11/46.

with the Yalta agreement are Soviet citizens are to cease forthwith.

All Soviet citizens are instructed to report at once to the Soviet Camp at Stuttgart. Those who do not report will be considered as having contravened Military Government orders, and will be seized here or in any other part of Germany occupied by the Americans, will be locked and will brought to Stuttgart under armed escort. This action is to come into effect to 0800 hours, d. 8/12/45.

Similarily orders have been issued to all foreign camps now in the American occupied zone. All local Burgomasters have been informed that Soviet citizens are not to be employed, and the German population must refuse them food.

For the benefit of those who wish to be transported to Stuttgart, transport lorries are available during the mornings of the 5th, 6th and 8th of December.

Stamp of the Mil. Gov. Det.
at Mannheim.

URGENT AND CONFIDENTIAL

MEMORANDUM
ON
"DIVISIA HALYCHYNA" A TOTAL OF ABOUT 9,000
SURRENDERED ENEMY PERSONNEL NOW IN RIMINI,
ITALY

Introduction.

In a Camp in Rimini, Italy, under the control of the British Army, there are held about 9,000 surrendered enemy personnel who were at one time in German uniform although they are not classified as prisoners of war. The full details on this Division together with the story behind its formation, the part that it played in the war as well as the reasons, are well known to the British Foreign Office and to the British War Office.

The Division was organised towards the end of the war from Ukrainian national, patriotic, humanitarian and religious reasons primarily in order to save Ukrainian youth from being conscripted into the regular German Forces to be used by the Germans at will and also in order to assure that in so much as it was humanly possible to prevent, the Ukrainians would not be used against the Western Allies. In both these respects some success was attained. Under the pretext of longer training and organising than was even reasonable, thousands of Ukrainian youth were saved from actual service in the German Forces and from useless sacrifice for a cause for which they had no love or respect. At the same time by a special agreement forced from the Germans, not a single one of the men in this Division was ever used in any shape or form in the West.

At the first possible opportunity this whole unit surrendered voluntarily to the British and American authorities.

Characteristics.

The chief characteristics of the personnel in this unit are:-

(A) they are all very strongly and permanently Western minded. Many of them have relatives and friends in Canada and the United States and in countries in South America.

(B) They are all religious. The majority are of the Eastern Catholic (Byzantine or Uniat) faith and are very strongly anti-Communist.

(C) They are all educated and developed in the Democratic way of life. This is chiefly due to the Polish citizenship which most of them had, to their relations and communications with their friends and relatives

137

in Canada and the United States prior to the war and to their general Christian principles and Western mindedness.

(D) The majority of them are excellent agricultural and industrial labourers and potential colonists. Most of them come from peasant stock.

(E) The bulk of them are young men between 18 and 30 years of age, strong, virile and healthy.

In consideration of the characteristics listed it is submitted that the personnel in this Camp at Rimini would make most excellent immigration material both from the point of view of colonisation and future citizenship and also from the point of view of any Western country's self-defence.

(3) Their future - indefinite and critical and solution urgent.

In the matter of a few weeks or months at the most, the Treaty with Italy will be signed. As soon as the Treaty is signed the British authorities will withdraw their forces from Italy. This group of surrendered enemy personnel, together with any others that may be in Italy, in the same or a similar position, will be left at the mercy of the Italian authorities. It is felt that the Italian Government will be subjected to severe pressure from the East. Both from economic and from political reasons it is feared that the Italian Government might submit to pressure from the East and that this group might be forcibly repatriated. From all Christian and humanitarian considerations this would be a great tragedy. It would also be from economic and political considerations a great loss to the Western World.

(4) Assistance by the international refugee organisation will not be granted.

According to the Charter of the I.R.O. this category of personnel come within the groups excluded from aid by the International Organisation, in keeping with the definitions in Annexe 1 of the Charter passed by the General Assembly. Any aid or assitance in any shape or form that could possibly be granted to these 9,000 victims of war whose future is so critical and uncertain must come from independent governments or organisations.

(5) Possible solutions.

(A) That these people be moved to some other place of asylum in a Western country more suitable than Italy as ordinary prisoners of

138

war or surrendered enemy personnel. In this capacity they could be used as labour for post war reconstruction.

(B) That the personnel of this unit be granted asylum in some country or countries if not permanently then for a definite period of time when they can be later moved or migrated again.

(C) That the personnel of this unit be granted special citizenship of the Vatican City or of some other country in order to make them eligible for immigration and to give them some form of legal status. Such legal status could also be obtained by some country recognising them as stateless and granting them asylum.

(D) That an opportunity be given to them to immigrate as ordinary immigrants (refugees or displaced persons) to some country in South America or North America, either as individuals, groups of individuals or as a unit, where they can settle and as naturalised citizens of the country of their asylum and adoption they can contribute to the growth and development of the country concerned.

Our voluntary Relief Organisations in Canada and the United States who are vitally interested in the fate of these victims of war are prepared to do everything in their power to provide or assist in providing the means of transportation for these people provided a place of asylum or immigration could be found.

From the strongest Christian and humanitarian principles of consideration and with the sincere object and desire to help solve a serious and critical post-war problem all the above is respectfully submitted.

> (B. PANCHUK)
> CENTRAL UKRAINIAN RELIEF BUREAU.

London, England, December 17th, 1946.

1. This camp consists entirely of male Ukrainians who were either captured in German uniform or were working in Germany as civilians and attached themselves to the 1st Ukrainian Division shortly before its surrender. The proportion of civilians is small, and doubt exists about exactly how many come into this category and about exactly when they joined up with the Division. I refer to this in more detail in paragraph 7 below. The number of inmates varies from time to time due to escapes, transfers to hospitals, etc., but the figure on which we have been working, and which was confirmed on 16th February by the British camp authorities as accurate, is a total of 8,272, which includes 218 permanently employed outside the camp on working parties. None had been screened previously by any British authority and no British records either on individuals or of a general nature were available to us here.

2. Individual screening by us being impossible, it was decided to question a small cross section chosen in accordance with their Wehrmacht formations. A full nominal roll broken up into these formations, was prepared for us by the Ukrainian camp leader, Major Jaskewycz, which gave the following breakdown:-

1203 Offrs and	ORs of the	1st Infantry Regt of the 1st Ukrainian Div.
1,058 ''	''	2nd Infantry Regt ''
1,150 ''	''	3rd Infantry Regt ''
938 ''	''	Artillery (actually with 4th Regt) ''
320 ''	''	Supply Section ''
305 ''	''	Engineer Bn. ''
205 ''	''	Signals Unit ''
2,230 ''	''	Recruiting Regt ''
76 ''	''	Workshop Coy. ''
281 ''	''	Fusilier Bn. ''
221 ''	''	Sanitary Section ''
156 ''	''	Anti Tank Section ''
125 ''	''	Divisional Staff ''
4 ''	''	Army Staff ''

8,272

3. At the same time Major Jaskewycz gave us his version of the history of the 1st Ukrainian Division and the various units that composed it. It

should be emphasized that all these nominal rolls and the short history of the Division were supplied entirely by the Ukrainians themselves and that we had no information here of any kind against which they could be checked; and virtually none of the menhad any identifying documents of any use, such as German Army pay books, though one or two of them had pre-war Polish civilian identity cards. I feel satisfied, however, that Major Jaskewycz has done his best to provide accurate and complete information, as far as he was able.

4. Our next step was to select a cross section of these people for questioning. We concentrated on the first three regiments and the Artillery Regiment in order to try and build up a Battle Order. 50 officers and men were chosen at random from the nominal rolls of these four regiments, but in actual practice it proved impossible to question only 47 of the 1st Regiment, 49 of the 2nd Regiment, 46 of the 3rd Regiment and 47 of the Artillery Regiment. A few others were chosen from the Signals Unit, the Supply Section and the Engineer Battalion, and 30 from the Recruiting or Reserve Regiment. Except in the case of Mr. Brown, who was able to question the men in Russian, Ukrainian speaking interpreters, who were actually inmates of the camp, had to be used.

5. When the questioning had been completed the individual statements of each man were checked against each other and against the information supplied by Major Jaskewycz about the Division and its various units. No serious discrepancies were discovered, nor did any particularly suspicious individual come to light, except in so far as some of them stated that they had volunteered for armed service with the Germans as early as July 1943, whereas the 1st Ukrainian Division does not appear to have been formed until the late summer of 1944. Nineteen men were therefore selected for further questioning, which disclosed that they had been enlisted in the summer of 1943 in the 1st Galician Division or the 14th Galician Grenadier Division. As it was not clear from the interrogations whether this was one and the same Division or two separate ones, I questioned the three senior officers in the Camp on this point, and established that it was called by the Germans the 14th Galician Waffen Grenadier Division and consisted of three Infantry and one Artillery Regiments. I do not see anything suspicious in some of the men not knowing exactly what unit they were in, and they probably referred to it as the 1st Galician Division because it was for them the first Division to be formed out of Ukrainians from Galicia. This Division suffered heavy losses at Brody in July 1944 and ceased to exist. The 1st Ukrainian Division was formed round its remnants. One of the officers of the 14th Galician Waffen Grenadier Division has stated that it was originally called by the Germans a Waffen SS Division but the SS was dropped from its title, on

141

the Ukrainians protesting, and that it subsequently became an ordinary German Army Division. It seems, however, to have had some SS training, which would account for some of its officers having given their ranks as "Untersturmfuehrer", which is an SS rank and not an ordinary German Army rank.

6. As far as the 1st Ukrainian Division is concerned, the short history supplied by Major Jaskewycz was borne out by the individual interrogations and we were able to draw up a nucleus of its Battle Order. The Division appears to have been formed about September 1944 and actually to have fought for only about one month in the late stages of the campaign in Austria (April 1945); the rest of its time was occupied in training and guard duties in Austria and Jugoslavia. It surrendered to us in Austria in May 1945. The men we questioned were nearly all of the simple peasant type, and made a good impression, showing no signs of either prevarication or truculence; a high proportion of them, and, from what we have seen, of the whole camp, are under 30 years of age. I myself questioned the three senior officers in the camp, Lt. Cols. Sylenko and Nikitin, and Major Jaskewycz. The other senior officers, namely two full colonels and one Lt. Col., were not available, but I feel sure that their story is similar to the history of the others. These three officers' stories were much the same. They were all born in the 1890's in Russia, became regular Tsarist army officers and fought in the 1914 war against the Germans. After the revolution of 1917 they fought for the Whites against the Bolsheviks in the Ukrainian Army: and when these hostilities came to an end all three settled in Poland as political emigrees with Nansen passports. None of them has this passport now, but Sylenko produced, as though it were a highly valuable objet d'art, a passport issued in 1918 by the Democratic Government of the Ukraine. He told me with pride that this was now very rare. They kept themselves in Poland from 1922 to 1939 by working in various civil jobs and continued in these jobs during and after the German occupation of Poland in 1939. They claimed that their status as political emigres exempted them from service in the Polish Army and all were insistent that they had never acquired Polish nationality. Some of the men, however, admit to having served in the Polish Army in 1939 and in a few cases were able to produce authentic looking documents in support of their claim to Polish nationality. No officer or man that we saw admitted to having served in the Red Army, nor do I think it likely that any of these Ukrainians did do so. About 10% are of the Orthodox faith. On the crucial point whether any of them are Soviet citizens by our definition we have no evidence other than that supplied by the men themselves. Many of the places which they have given as their place of birth and/or habitual residence

142

are small villages and hamlets which are not likely to be marked on any but the largest maps; but I think we can safely assume that the great majority of those born after 1919 were born in Poland, and were resident in Poland on 1st September 1939, and that the great majority of those born before Poland existed were not resident in the Soviet Union on 1st September 1939. The general impression which we have formed of all the men in the camp is favourable, as they strike us all as being decent, simple minded sort of people. The national emblem of the Ukraine, in the form of a trident, is freely displayed all over the camp, and the inmates clearly regard themselves as a homogeneous unit, unconnected either with Russia or Poland, and do not seem conscious of having done any wrong.

7. Our attention has been concentrated on trying to build up a Battle Order and a general picture of the Division, and we have for this reason paid no attention to any of the miscellaneous units except the Signals Unit, the Supply Section, and the Engineer Battalion. Some of the real villains of the piece, if there are any, may be sheltering behind these innocuous sounding units, but that is a risk which we have to take. We did, however, question 30 of the Recruiting or Reserve Regiment, the largest single unit in the camp. We did not expect these interrogations to throw much light on the Division as a whole, which proved to be the case; but we were anxious to question some men in this regiment, as the camp leader had told us that a fair proportion of them were really civilians such as Todt workers, who had only attached themselves to the regiment shortly before its surrender, as a means of escaping from the Germans. It so happened that of the 30 men we picked, none admitted to having been a Todt worker, although six of them said that they had not been enlisted in the regiment until the early part of 1945, and that before this date they had been working in various factories in Germany. Time prevented us from pursuing the matter further, but this omission is not important, as if any of the men were really civilians that must be considered a point in their favour rather than the reserve.

8. During the course of our enquiries we discovered that nearly all these Ukrainians had already been screened by an official Soviet Mission (they were then in a different camp at Bellaria). The first part of the Soviet Mission arrived on 13th August 1945, with the primary object of weeding out all the Ukrainians who were not Soviet citizens according to the Soviet definition, by which all people who were resident in that part of pre-war Poland bounded on the west by the Curzon line and on the east by the then Polish-Soviet frontier were considered Soviet citizens if they were still resident in that area by the time the Red Army occupied it in late September 1949(?). 397 officers and men who had claimed not to

143

be Soviet citizens, were screened by the Soviet Mission and 127 of them were passed as not being Soviet citizens and were forthwith removed from the Ukrainian camp (most of them are now back in it). The remainder were kept in the camp. On 17th August 1945 Col. Jakovlev arrived in order to discuss administrative matters. He maintained that all those left in the camp after the Soviet screening should be administered on lines laid down by the Soviet Union, and that they were eligible for the scale of rations, clothing and pay to which free Soviet citizens were entitled under the Yalta agreement. This contention was rejected. Colonel Jaloclev thereupon decided to begin a drive in the camp for voluntary repatriation, and to break down the general resistance to such repatriation by having what he called the "stubborn Fascist minority removed from the camp. A supplementary Soviet Mission under General Vasilov arrived on the 20th August for this purpose, but only succeeded in securing 50 volunteers for repatriation, who were forthwith removed from the camp and reclassified as Free Soviet citizens. They are presumably back in the Soviet Union. The General and his personal staff left the camp on the 25th August, having met with a hostile reception and having apparently abandoned any further attempt to secure more volunteers. The task which General Vasilov had begun of identifying the stubborn Fascist minority was continued by the original members of the mission who had arrived on the 13th August and was not completed until the end of September. Some attempt was made at thoroughness in dealing with the officers, but most of the men appear to have been treated in a remarkably high handed and abrupt manner. When the mission had finished they stated to the British authorities that a minority in the camp was definitely responsible for terrorising the great majority from volunteering for repatriation, and that once this minority had been removed from the camp most of the remainder would eventually come forward as volunteers. 11 men were in fact removed at the request of the Soviet Mission, but were subsequently allowed by the British authorities to return. I am satisfied that there are no grounds for the Soviet Mission's complaint of terrorisation. No official report of their activities was supplied by the Soviet Mission to the local British authorities, and the information given in this paragraph was supplied by Major Hills, GSI(b) of this Sub-Area, who was present when the visits took place.

9. The only effect, which the Soviet Mission's visit appears to have had on the Ukrainians, was to convince any waverers there might have been never to return to the Soviet Union, and to cause a great deal of probably justified anxiety to those who still had relatives there. We must, I think, accept as a definite fact, that all those Ukrainians now in Camp 374 who were screened by the Soviet Mission—that is to say the great majority—

are now regarded by the Soviet Government as Soviet citizens, and that having failed to secure their voluntary repatriation the Soviet Government will demand their forcible repatriation as War Criminals when the Italian Treaty comes into force.

10. Attached you will find the following results or our activities:-

+   i. Nominal rolls of all the inmates of the camp broken up into their various Wehrmacht Units.
   ii. Information about each unit supplied by Major Jaskewycz.
  iii. Names of those chosen for questioning.
  iv. Case sheets of the results of this questioning (enclosed in a separate folder).
   v Summary of information taken from cases.
  vi. Battle Order for the first three Regiments, the Artillery Regiment and the Recruiting Regiment compiled from the individual questionnaires and from Major Jaskewycz's histories.

+   Note: These are not forwarded with this report.

11. We have thus obtained a reasonably consistant picture as far as it goes, and as far as it can go within the limits of our time and resources. The men may be all or in part lying, and even their names may be false. No attempt at cross examination was made except where some obscurity of glaring discrepancy was revealed during the course of the interrogation; the work in fact which the screeners have done has largely consisted of taking down through an interpreter the men's answers to a limited number of set questions. If, however, we are to get anywhere we must, and in my opinion, can safely, assume that by and large the men are what they say they are and did what they say they did. It would seem therefore that the only further screening processes that can usefully be applied:

   i. To see if any of the men listed in the nominal rolls figure in UNWCC or CROWCASS lists or have been specifically accused by the Russian or other Government of War Crimes
  ii. To see if any of the units to which the men belong have particularly bad war records.
  iii. To see if the short history of the various units and of the Division as a whole, as ascertained by interrogation, corresponds to the known facts about them. It might be possible to locate some of the German officers of the Division and have them questioned. None are known to be in this area.

If this further screening confirms the history of the units and produces no bad units and no wanted men, then the solution of the problem resolves itself into taking a decision on the following general considerations.

A. It seems likely that the great majority, at least of the men, are not Soviet citizens by our definition. It must, however, be borne in mind that an official Soviet Mission has questioned nearly all of them, and that the Soviet Government merely regards nearly all of them as Soviet citizens; and that there *may* be among them a number who are Soviet citizens by our definition. We may therefore, if we get them all accepted as D.Ps render ourselves liable to a valid charge of sheltering Russian traitors. (It might be worth while noting in this connection that on the nationality issue these men are really having the best of both worlds. They do not qualify as Soviet citizens because their place of birth and/or habitual domicile on 1.9.39 were in Poland, and they therefore by our definition escape all punishment by the Russians for their having assisted the enemy; and they are not presumably eligible now for punishment by the Polish authorities because that part of the country from which they came is no longer part of Poland).

B. The great majority of them voluntarily enlisted in the German Armed Forces and fought against our Allies, Soviet Russia and Jugoslavia. There are some grounds for believing that some of those whom we have questioned have stated that they were volunteers, because if they said that they had been conscripted they would then be told that they would have nothing to fear if they returned to the Ukraine. The number of volunteers may thus be smaller than would at first appear. None the less, also allowing for intimidation, dislike of forced labour, the majority for our purpose must be regarded as volunteers. There are, therefore, prima facie grounds for classifying them as traitors, i.e. as ineligible for I.R.O. status according to the 1st section of paragraph two of the definition sheet. The term 'traitor' is vague and has been defined for our guidance by Professor Royse as embodying, among other things, 'civilians who voluntarily offer their services to the enemy and, in general sense, people who gave aid and comfort to the enemy'. This definition undoubtedly applies to most, if not all, of these Ukrainians.

C. We must however I think take into account their motives for having voluntarily offered their services to the enemy, even though by so doing one might be able, as a reductio absurdum, to prove Quisling himself as eligible for I.R.O. assistance. There seem to be four main reasons for their having taken this step.

    (a) The hope of securing a genuinely independent Ukraine.

146

(b) Without knowing exactly what they were doing, e.g. because other Ukrainians whom they knew had already volunteered.

(c) As a preferable alternative to forced labour etc., or to living in Soviet controlled territory.

(d) To have a smack at the Russians, whom they always refer to as 'Bolsheviks'.

They probably were not, and certainly do not now seem to be at heart pro-German, and the fact that they did give aid and comfort to the Germans can fairly be considered to have been incidental and not fundamental.

D. The desire among their leaders for an independent Ukraine, naive and unreal as it is, is none the less genuine.

E. They are obsessed by a terror and hatred, bordering in some cases almost on hysteria, of Soviet Russia. It seems clear that when the Russians occupied Eastern Poland in 1939/40 many of these people's wives and families were ruthlessly taken away from their homes to Siberia and other remote parts of the Soviet Union and have not been seen or heard of since. They also seem to have suffered a good deal at the hands of the Red Army during the Russo-German campaign, and also on occasions at the hands of the Germans.

F. None of them wish to return to the Ukraine, with the exception of one man, who, after securing an interview with one of the Commissioners and stating to him that he did wish to return to the Ukraine, was subsequently found to be suffering from the last stages of consumption and was not expected to live very much longer. He is now in hospital.

G. No one in the camp has been sentenced by any British military authority to one year's imprisonment or over. Their behaviour indeed since their surrender to us has been exemplary. They have not indulged in any subversive activities, nor do I thing they will do so in the future. They seem resigned to the fact that there is now no place in Europe for them and that those of them who have wives and families in Soviet Union will never see them again. We must not, however, expect most of them ever to become well disposed towards the Soviet Union.

12. I am not competent from here to judge the issue as far as our relations with the Soviet Union (or with Poland) are concerned; nor do I know whether our policy is to interpret strictly or liberally the instructions as to who is eligible for DP status and who not. I can only speak from the experience gained from our actually having seen the men and

147

from humanitarian instincts common to us all; and on this basis and taking into account the long time that has elapsed from the end of the war, I recommend most strongly that all these Ukrainians should be classified as DPs; and I would add, with all the emphasis I can command, that, if this is accepted, immediate action, not high-sounding resolutions, is necessary either to ensure that the I.R.O. or the I.G.C.R. can give them effective protection as DPs from being handed over to the Soviet Government by the Italian Government under the Treaty, or to have them removed lock, stock and barrel from Italy before the Treaty comes into force.

(sgd). D. HALDANE PORTER
Refugee Screening Commission
In charge S.E.P. Camp 374.

ASSOCIATION OF UKRAINIANS IN GREAT BRITAIN, LTD.
(Registered under the War Charities Act 1940)

49 Linden Gardens, Notting Hill Gate, London, W. 2.
England.   8th April, 1948.

Dear Sirs,

RELEASE AND RESETTLEMENT OF RIMINI GROUP. (Previously S.E.P. in Italy and now P.o.W. in U.K.)

After a long period of waiting and endless efforts, pressure, pleas and intervention, the fundamental principles for the release and resettlement of this particular category of Ukrainian war victims, which numbers over 8,500 persons, is now established. Following are the main conditions of release.

1. Ukrainian prisoners of war now in Great Britain will be released and demobilised as voluntary workers in exactly the same character as those workers at present volunteering in Germany and Austria for employment in Great Britain. At the time of release they will be issued with civilian documents on which there will be no record or remarks of any kind whatsoever to indicate that they had been prisoners of war. However, all Ukrainians who were prisoners of war and who voluntarily accepted employment in the U.K. and take their discharge are restricted to employment in the agricultural industry.

2. All Ukrainian PW Camps will be visited by representatives from the Ministry of Labour and/or the Ministry of Agriculture, who will carry

out a form of recruiting and selection. All selected voluntary workers, after having been accepted, will be medically examined and will be required to sign a commitment and undertaking similar to that which is being signed by the voluntary workers selected in Germany and Austria.

3. The British Government fears and regrets that, unless some other convenient solution can be found, all those who are at present ill or confined to hospitals or unfit for labour for one reason or another, will be repatriated to Germany.

4. The British Government does not accept any responsibility and will make no commitments with respect to bringing to Great Britain the families or dependants of those who may accept discharge and employment in Great Britain.

5. The transition period from their present status of PW to their civilian status will be gradual and is expected to take a few months, depending on demands for labour and accommodation facilities.

6. All those who make any arrangements or who have any possibility of immigrating to Canada or the United States will be permitted to immigrate after civilianisation. That is to say, there will be no obstructions whatsoever raised by the British authorities regardless of the undertaking that they will have signed upon discharge. All those who have any possibilities of immigrating to any country in South America or to any country in Europe or elsewhere and who can give assurance that transportation is available and produces authorisations for visas, will be immediately documented and permitted to immigrate. The British Government, however, will undertake no commitment for transportation and it is up to the individuals themselves or authorised voluntary agencies or committees to cover the costs of transportation.

7. There is no question whatsoever concerning forced repatriation anywhere for anybody except, as has also already been stated, for those who are seriously ill and unfit for employment. These at present are under the threat of repatriation to Germany so as to be loaded off on to the German economy. All Ukrainians PWs, regardless of their geographical origin (whether Western or Eastern Ukraine) may rest assured that all danger of repatriation has now passed.

It is desirable to add here that, based on conversations with officials in the various Ministries of the British Government concerned, they have no objection whatsoever to the Ukrainians remaining here or to their emigrating onward if they have the possibility. It is difficult, however, to persuade the Home Office, which is the first Ministry concerned directly, to assume the burden and responsibility of keeping and maintaining the sick, the invalids and those who are unfit for employment. This group consists specifically of the following categories.

a) 238 soldiers very seriously ill confined to three military hospitals numbers 162, 99 and 231.

b) 122 temporarily ill who are confined to various sick bays in the different camps.

c) About 156 cripples, invalids and elderly persons, some of whom are completely unfit for physical labour, others are unfit for heavy labour but could manage in lighter duties.

This roughly gives a figure of 500 Ukrainians who are threatened with repatriation to Germany. The fate that they can expect in Germany is well known to all of us. Who will give them the necessary care and maintenance? The Germans certainly will not assume any responsibility for these "foreigners". What will happen to them should any changes come about in the occupation arrangements? What is their hope or possibility of immigration anywhere. Taking all possibilities into consideration, it is certain and obvious that they are doomed to a slow and torturous death and liquidation. Heavy responsibility lies upon every Ukrainian who is settled in employment and who is earning whatever it may happen to be. It is estimated that if we were to take complete responsibility for these people upon our own shoulders, organising our own private hospital with our own doctors and staff (which can easily be done), a very minimum budget of 10,000 dollars a month is required to start with. Can the Ukrainians living and employed in Western Europe, in Great Britain, in Canada and the United States, provide this money? In what ratio of importance are these 500 people who have offered practically the supreme sacrifice and who are now doomed only because fate brought sickness upon them in addition to their other sufferings. Their sacrifice for the cause of freedom and in the battle against communism is equal, and perhaps much greater, than the sacrifice of any soldier who fought during the war in the Allied Forces.

Action must be immediately started in order to persuade the British Home Office to permit these men to remain in the United Kingdom and to remove for ever the threat of their repatriation to Germany or any other country where it would be humanly impossible for us to give them the help that they so rightly deserve.

Action must, however, be started immediately and the general campaign set in motion in order to obtain funds in order to give these people the care and maintenance that they so rightly deserve. The comrades of these unfortunates from among their fellow prisoners of war, those who are stronger and healthier and whose chances of employment and free-

150

dom have now been assured, have already agreed to tax. themselves at a rate of 1/—per week (1 dollar per month) for as long as it may be required, and if necessary for ever, until such time as these men require that help. Obviously, these payments can only be made after the soldiers concerned have taken on employment. There is no doubt about it, that the Ukrainian Voluntary Workers who have come to Great Britain from Germany and Austria will also tax themselves in a similar manner and perhaps an equal ratio. Based on the highest expectations and the greatest faith in our fellow countrymen, we can count on only 50% of them being able to honour their commitment. We are forced, therefore, to appeal to all Ukrainians in Canada and all Ukrainians in Great Britain, to our churches, to our organised committees, to all society wherever it may be and to all our friends among the British, among the Canadian and among the American citizens, to give to us that help. We are forced to appeal to every human being who has any sense of appreciation for what these men have suffered and sacrificed in the past. Practically every one of them has lost his entire home and family to the unparalleled destruction spread by the communists. Their only hope for the future are their fellow countrymen who were fortunate enough to have reached Canada or the United States or have come to Great Britain. Their only further hope is in all those non-Ukrainians but friends of all suffering mankind who can understand the plight of the refugees, displaced persons and unfortunate victims of war following this last war. Any assistance that you or any of your friends can give us in this present urgency,

a) by sending cables and petitions to the British Home Office in order to persuade the British Government that these unfortunates be permitted to remain in the U.K., and

b) in order to gather funds and press hard a compaign which will provide us with the ways and means of guaranteeing care and maintenance and medical attention for these unfortunates,

would be sincerely and gratefully appreciated.

Yours
(G.R.B. Panchuk).

Memorandum
re:
UKRAINIAN "DIVISIA HALYCHYNA", (UKRAINIAN P.O.W. IN GREAT BRITAIN), PREVIOUSLY "SURRENDERED ENEMY PERSONNEL" IN RIMINI, ITALY.

Part I. Introduction.

It is necessary and desirable to place on record certain fundamental facts and information concerning this particular group of war victims who constitute a particular category in themselves.

It is hoped that the information herein contained will prove of value and of interest and will aid in gaining favourable consideration with regard to the suggestions and recommendations made in the conclusion.

Part II. Historical Background.

1. The Division was organised towards the end of the war by the Germans in circumstances well known to everybody, exploiting in particular the natural and inborn anti-communist and anti-Russian feelings and convictions of the Ukrainians.

2. When it appeared inevitable that the Germans would organise such a Unit, leading and outstanding Ukrainians for national, patriotic, humanitarian and religious reasons, interested themselves in the Unit in as much as it was possible for them to do so.

3. The first conversations that the Germans had with the Ukrainians concerning the formation of such a Unit were in March 1943. Prior to that, the only Ukrainians serving with the German forces were:

    a)   individuals scattered throughout various German Units who had been drawn in between the period 1941 to 1943,

and

    b)   the so-called "Ukrainian Legion" which constituted a battalion of about 800 persons formed originally illegally and underground in 1940-41 preparatory for the Russian-German clash. In 1941 small parts of this Legion were legalized and came to Galicia with the "regional" units of the German Wehrmacht.

Note: The conviction among all Ukrainians at that time was that the Germans would assist, or if not assist then at least tolerate, the establishment of an "independent Ukraine". This, however, was soon proved to be a false hope. The "temporary Government" which established itself in 1941 (without public support) was disbanded, all leading nationalists were arrested or liquidated and the remnants of the "Ukrainian Legion" were disbanded, arrested and placed into concentration camps. Those who managed to get away went underground into the Ukrainian partisan army.

4. The first announcements of the formation of the Ukrainian Division "Halychyna" were made to the Ukrainians in May 1943 by the Ukrainian Central Committee. In the first announcements it was clearly pointed out that the Unit was the beginning of the Ukrainian National Army and that the service was for the Ukraine. A popular motto used in the recruiting was "if you are being given arms — take them". Another was, "take advantage of your only opportunity to destroy communism and free your native land".

5. The appeals were directed firstly and primarily to the Ukrainian war veterans of the 1918-1922 independence struggle and it was these veterans who formed the nucleus of the Unit.

6. Posts were established throughout Galicia by the Germans where "volunteers" could submit their applications. The methods in which young men were "recruited" and the motives which prompted or persuaded men to join this Unit are dealt with in more detail further in this memorandum. The Germans insisted, however, that regardless of how the man happened to be "recruited" and regardless of what the motives, reasons or circumstances, he was compelled to sign an "application form" declaring that he "voluntarily applied to serve in Divisia Halychyna".

7. Recruiting was restricted mostly to Ukrainians from Galicia and mostly from the districts around Lviv. The chosen emblem for the Division was the Lion which is the historical and national emblem of the Province of Galicia (Lviv). Only later was recruiting extended to take in Ukrainians from other regions and territories.

8. On July 17th the first transport of about 2,000 was despatched for training to Czechoslovakia. Training was conducted by the Germans in German training centres.

9. In November 1943, two companies were despatched for training in France in the Bay of Biscay regions which, after training, were brought back and stationed in the area around Tarnopol.

10. By agreement made between the Ukrainian leaders and the German high command, *the Ukrainian Division was to be used only and exclusively on the Eastern Front against the Russians*. This agreement was publicly announced and proclaimed and is on record as announced by Himmler on the instructions of Hitler. Records of the proclamation are still available in the Vatican.

11. The oath required to be taken by the Ukrainians was (freely translated), "I swear before God and my native land to continue the fight against communism to the bitter end...."

12. In March 1944 the Division was beginning to take form. The smaller units which were scattered for training purposes in various parts of Czechoslovakia were assembled together at NEUHAMMER in Western Poland (SCHLESEN near BRESLAU). In accordance with the general policy for all non-German "foreign" units, the unit was termed Waffen S.S. This should not, however, be mistaken for the actual German S.S. in which only "pure bred" Germans could serve. The Ukrainians were permitted to have priests in their units, they were not given any S.S. identity marks whatsoever and the terminology of their ranks and titles were those of the Wehrmacht.

13. In June 1944 the first and only "pre-action" manoeuvres were held at Neuhammer. It was during these manoeuvres at a conference of all officers when Himmler proclaimed the agreement made that "the Feuhrer had consented to the demand of the Ukrainian Committee and agreed that the Ukrainian Division Halychyna would be used only and exclusively on the Eastern Front against the communists".

14. The Division was incorporated into the Second Corps of the German Wehrmacht and on July 14th 1944 sent to the front lines and took part in its one and only major action at Brody, East of Lviv in Galicia. At this time, the unit consisted of about 14,000 men, together with a reserve of about 2,000. It was during this period, one will recall, that the first signs of breakdown in the German political and war machine were evident. This was the period of the attempted attack on Hitler, the beginning of the major Russian offensive, the period when large numbers of German units were crossing over both to the Russian side on the east and to the Allies on the west.

15. In the Battle at Brody, most of the Germans, as a result of the chaos and conflicting reports which came down concerning the attempted attack on Hitler, deserted the front line units and pulled out. The Ukrainian Division was left alone to hold the line and in the battle was practically annihilated. Many were destroyed in action; many were captured by the Russians and immediately destroyed and massacred; a very small number, after being taken prisoner, managed to save their lives by pretending to be Germans, (Ukrainians were automatically killed and were not taken prisoners); many committed suicide and a very large number went underground to join the Ukrainian partisan units in the Carpathian mountains. About 3,000 of the entire 16,000 managed to save themselves and broke through, reassembled themselves gradually via Kracow and points in Hungary at Neuhammer.

154

16. Upon their return to Neuhammer, they were all placed in concentration by the Germans who considered and treated them as "traitors".

17. During the last part of August and the early part of September 1944, instructions were received to form a new Division and fresh reserves were brought up from the "recuits" who were still being assembled from everywhere.

18. For this "Second Division" the recruiting campaign was "all out" and spread in every direction. Ukrainians who had been serving individually in other German units were all transferred to the Division whether they wanted to or not. There was "all out" recruiting from labour camps in Germany, Austria and all parts of Western Europe occupied by the Germans, as well as from concentration camps in Germany and Austria, etc., and every means and method was used to compel every Ukrainian physically fit to join the unit. It will be remembered that during this particular period the Germans were very hardpressed for manpower (for the Eastern front in particular) and all "alien" and non-German manpower was being mobilized to the utmost.

19. Training continued during the latter part of September and the early part of October. On September 23rd one battalion of the unit was moved to Slovakia where they continued training and in addition their job was to recruit "volunteers" from the Slovak partisans to the Wehrmacht.

20. It is desirable at this point to clear up a fallacy which intentionally or unintentionally is spread, to the effect that the Ukrainian Division was used by the Germans to help crush the Warsaw uprising. This is a complete fallacy and cannot be substantiated since from every point of view it was physically impossible for the Ukrainians to have taken part *in any action whatsoever during that period*. The uprising took place on August 28th 1944 which was shortly after the Battle of Brody. During the time of the rising the Ukrainian Division had just gone through its annihilation and scattered units and individuals were making their way chaotically back to Neuhammer for reorganisation. The Division was *not* reorganised in *any* form until during the latter part of September

21. During the months of October, November and December, and the early part of January, the entire Division was gradually moved to Slovakia to continue training. They remained there until the latter part of January 1945.

22. On January 27th, general evacuation started westward in the direction of Vienna and the Province of Corinthia in Austria. In Austria the unit continued training and was also used in mopping up operations against the Tito partisans. The unit remained in Austria from early February until the capitulation in May.

155

23. During this period, a number of attempts were made to cross over to the British who were coming up from Italy and contacts were established with the British forces. After one such attempt in March, the Germans disarmed the entire unit and placed them under concentration, but with the approach of the Red Army arms were returned.

24. On April 8th, the united was again in minor action against the Red Army at Feldbach and area.

25. On May 8th the unit was successful in crossing to join the British forces and on May 6th the first official meeting was held with British officers at Klagenfort. The surrender took place at Klagenfort, Feldkirchen and other points in the Province of Corinthia. Arms were not removed from the unit; in fact, in many cases more arms were issued and the unit was instructed to cross over to Italy. The move beginning on May 28th ended up (via Udine, Balaria, etc.), at Rimini.

Part III. Methods and Sources of Recruiting and Criteria for "Volunteering".

1. It is a historical fact that the Ukrainians have always strived for their political independence and have endeavoured to take advantage of every opportunity which might give them the slightest hope of making a contribution towards the independence of Ukraine. These efforts were best exemplified during the period 1918-1922 when the independent Ukraine *was* established and recognised.

2. A fair number of World War I veterans took advantage of the opportunity to get arms and ammunition and additional military training in order to fight against the communists which were always considered as the greater of two evils.

3. A very large number of youth were encouraged to take advantage of the opportunity to get arms, ammunition and training in order to subsequently join the underground partisans.

4. Until the outbreak of war in 1941 the Ukrainians were equally considered by the Russians (Eastern Ukraine), the Poles (Western Ukraine) and by the Germans themselves, as a dissident element that could not be trusted and, therefore, they were not admitted into any of the regular units for military service. Ukrainians took advantage of the first and only opportunity available and possibly hoping thus to form the nucleus of a Ukrainian Army, as they had after the first World War, in order to continue the struggle for Ukrainian independence.

5. Slave workers in Germany "volunteered" in order to take advantage of the only opportunity to get out of the slave labour camps.

156

6. Peasants and the sons of peasants "volunteered" so as not to be "home" when the Russians returned, having already experienced Russian occupation in 1939 41.

7. Young men "volunteered" in order to escape being drafted into other German units since the Germans were mobilizing all youth physically fit.

8. Those who were in concentration camps or who were threatened with concentration camps "volunteered", to escape from the threat or the camp.

9. Ukrainian prisoners of war held by the Germans were offered the opportunity to "volunteer" to go into the Ukrainian Division.

10. Ukrainians who had previously been drafted to other German units were offered the opportunity to "volunteer" for transfer from these German units to the Ukrainian Division.

11. An organised secret plan and agreement existed among the Ukrainians themselves whereby Ukrainians from the underground partisan army "volunteered" to join the Division, took training and deserted again.

12. Frequent raids were conducted by the Germans throughout the Ukraine and all young men picked up during such raids were given the choice of either slave labour in Germany or to "volunteer" for service in the Division.

13. Civilian stragglers and camp followers attached themselves to the Division during the move from Slovakia to Austria in order to evacuate themselves before the approaching Red Army.

14. Special "privileges" and the right of evacuation for families and dependants were offered as an incentive to tempt and to encourage sons and husbands to "volunteer" to preserve and save their families and dependants.

15. During their time in Slovakia, young boys who had previously been mobilized for "Fatherland Service" in such duties as anti-aircraft, pioneer corps, light general duties, etc., were transferred to the Division and given an opportunity to "volunteer".

16. German Police and Wehrmacht made regular and periodic raids on villages, searched for youth and drove them away in lorries to "volunteer" for slave labour or military service.

17. During the German retreat, it was the policy of the Germans to forcibly evacuate all males before them. These were either mobilized on the spot during the evacuation or concentrated in points and then mobilized. All of these were given an opportunity to "volunteer". All

Ukrainian "partisans" who were captured by the Germans were faced with immediate execution or given the opportunity to "volunteer" for the Division.

18. A few thousand stragglers, camp followers and deserters from slave labour camps and other working units in Austria, attached themselves to the unit after capitulation in order to take advantage of the opportunity to cross over into Italy.

19. Many Ukrainians from the Polish Army in Italy deserted to join their own nationals, preferring to suffer the same fate, and often to join their relatives or close friends. No doubt a certain number of individual "fortune hunters" and adventurers "volunteered" for domestic reasons, for personal reasons, in order to find some "hope" for "security" for themselves or for their families and dependants or because they had nowhere else to go and no other alternative.

Part IV. Statistics and Chief Characteristics.

1. *INTRODUCTION* On the basis of a survey conducted recently, certain information concerning the various camps in the United Kingdom where Ukrainians are located might prove of interest. It should be pointed out that while the informations is not final and complete, it does give a fairly good overall picture of the chief characteristics.

2. The final date of the survey is March 3rd 1948. At that date there were 8,361 Ukrainian POW in the U.K. They were distributed throughout camps and hostels as follows:-

Camp No. 16, Haddington,	-965,	Camp No. 85,	Bly,	-296,
Camp No. 17, Sheffield,	- 73,	Camp No. 85,	Cheveley,	- 88,
Camp No. 51, Allington,	-595,	Camp No. 85,	Saham,	- 50,
Camp No. 53, Sherburn,	-139,	Hosp. No. 99,	Shugborough Park,	-84,
Camp No. 56, Botesdale,	-840,	Camp No. 122,	Scrubs Lane,	- 18,
Camp No. 79, Tattershall Thorpe,	-474,	Camp No. 153,	Spalding,	- 50,
Camp No. 82, Fakenham,	-878,	Camp No. 156,	Wellingore,	-698,
Camp No. 82, Cooley Cley,	-551,	Hosp. No. 162,	Naburn,	-104,
Camp No. 82, Langham,	-180,	Hosp. No. 231,	Redgrave Park,	- 99,
Camp No. 82, Matlaske,	-346,	Hosp. No. 232,	Blockley,	- 5,
Camp No. 85, Victoria,	-462,	Camp No. 249,	Carburton,	-625,
Camp No. 85, West Tofts,	-293,	Camp No. 298,	Barony Camp,	-452.

3. According to qualifications and professions of the various camps, the following roughly was the distribution:-

Agricultural workers		-4,322
Ordinary unskilled labour		- 816

Technicians and skilled workers	-2,216
Tradesmen	- 89
Teachers	- 91
Administrators	- 147
Other trades	680

4. As an additional supplementary survey, there is the attached appendix showing in detail the various trades and skills available.

5. Classification according to age:-

Under 20 years	- 44
Between 20 and 25 years	-3,341
Between 25 and 30 years	-2,586
Between 30 and 40 years	-1,574
Between 40 and 50 years	- 456
Over 50 years	- 110
Unknown (information not available)	- 250

6. Information concerning dependants, close relatives and next-of-kin figures given refer to PWs.

Those who have:-

(a) Dependants and close relatives in the Ukraine or in various other territories of the USSR (Siberia, etc.),	-4,914
(b) Dependants and close relatives in other countries under Soviet occupation,	- 873
(c) Dependants in Germany,	- 364
(d) Dependants in Austria,	- 80
(e) Dependants in other European countries,	- 145
(f) Dependants in Canada,	- 649
(g) Dependants in U.S.A.,	- 312
(h) Dependants in Argentine,	- 147
(i) In other non-European countries,	- 48
Without dependants or immediate close relatives,	- 579
Unknown, (information not available),	- 250

7 The following is a classification according to marital status:-

Married and having children	-1,327
Married, without children	- 498
Unmarried	-6,286
Not known	- 250

8. According to religion the following is the classification:-

Ukrainian Greek Catholic (Uniat)	-7,234
Ukrainian Greek Orthodox (Autocephalic)	- 860
Other religions	- 17
Unknown (no information)	- 250

9. It is interesting to note how the study of the English language has improved since the last survey made in October. At present the picture is somewhat as follows:-

Those who know English well	- 232
Those who know well enough to read and understand	- 835
Those who are studying it and know elementary principles	-2,600

10. Classification according to health was as follows:-

Seriously ill, some long term	-170
Mild illness	-135
Invalids and those partially or wholly unfit for heavy labour	-182
Total	487

Note Since their arrival in the U.K. 12 persons have died. 117 persons have been "repatriated" on their own request to Germany.

11. The following was the picture with regard to employment:-

Those employed in physical labour outside of camps	-4,262
Those employed in camp administration	-1,434
No information concerning	- 965

12. *Social, Cultural and Spiritual Welfare.*

a) Throughout the camps available for the use of the PWs was a total of 20 church chapels, 17 theatrical halls, 21 suitable halls for reading rooms, etc., 13 suitable sports grounds, two suitable classrooms, 2 billiard halls. In addition to these, 7 different camps had permanent organised exhibitions of arts and handicraft.

b) 19 camps or hostels had libraries, (no information is available from 5 camps). These libraries contained a total of 2,979 Ukrainian books, 2,537 English books, 2,739 German books and smaller quantities of books in other languages.

c) Among the enterprises organised and operated by the men were 13 choirs, 11 orchestras, 6 dramatic groups, 5 dance ballets, 7 wood carving clubs, 14 football teams, 2 ping-pong teams, as well as various competitions in chess, etc.

d) Since their arrival in the U.K., the following entertainment has been organised and provided:-

65 concerts and festivals,
36 stage and dramatic revues,

525 picture shows,
205 speeches and 32 shows provided by guest artists.

In addition to these, the PWs have given a total of over 25 concerts for charity and welfare purposes to voluntary workers and to the British public, usually sponsored and organised by the local churches, neighbouring EVW hostels or by the Association of Ukrainians in Great Britain.

e) 8 camps have their editorial boards and publish bi-monthly journals in the Ukrainian language, 2 camps have organised daily radio broadcast of news to every hut and one camp publishes its wall newspaper.

f) No *permanent* educational courses were conducted but 18 camps held fairly regular courses for teaching English, 3 camps operated courses to teach driving and chaffeuring, 4 camps had organised self education and social welfare, 1 camp operated a secondary school, 2 camps conducted studies of English literature, 1 camp organised a study group in history, 1 operated a study circle in physics and mathematics and 1 operated a class in national folk dancing.

13. *Emigration* The following were the emigration sentiments shown by the men:-

a) Voluntarily preferring to remain in the United Kingdom,   -2,618
b) To immigrate to countries in Western Europe,   - 296
c) To immigrate to Canada,   -2,980
   (only 644 have the necessary affidavits of support)
d) To immigrate to U.S.A.,   -1,185
   (only 365 have the necessary affidavits of support)
e) To immigrate to Argentine,   - 551
   (only 55 have the necessary affidavits of support)
f) To immigrate to other countries,   - 186
   (of these 8 had affidavits of support)
g) Undecided,   - 545

14. *General Characteristics*.

a) All the men are very strongly and permanently Western minded and fairly well educated and developed in the democratic way of life as understood in the West. This is chiefly due to the large number of relatives and friends in Canada, the United States and in countries in South America, and also to the fact that most of them ere pre-war Polish citizens (Ukrainian Province of Galicia). Their religious Catholic training also had bearing on these characteristics.

b) They are all very religious, mostly of the Eastern Catholic (Byzantine rite). Their demands for spiritual welfare surpass all our means and abilities to provide these services.

161

c) Politically they are almost violently anti-communist and opposed to all forms of autocratic Government. They have practically all experienced Russian occupation during the period 1939-41 and practically everyone has suffered directly (either personally or through his family) from the communist regime in the USSR. Although slightly to a lesser degree, they equally dislike the Germans and the Poles — for the same historical reasons.

d) The majority are of peasant stock with agricultural training or experience to a greater or lesser degree. All of them are potential settlers and colonists.

Part V. Effects of the Past Three Years.

1. The Division crossed over from Austria to Italy during the latter part of May and the early part of June 1945. While about 2,000 or so stragglers, camp followers and workers from labour camps, etc., attached themselves to the unit in order to get across to Italy, a large number of soldiers from the Division itself did *not* go the Italy but stayed behind in Austria. Of these about 5,000 went straight into civilian life and became DPs, having joined with their families or relatives or friends who had also evacuated westward as refugees, while about another 3,000 were taken by the Americans as POW, kept as POW from a minimum of 6 months to a maximum of 1 year and subsequently released as civilians. These latter also became DPs and went into DP camps.

2. Of those who went across to Italy and were subsequently interned in the SEP cage at Rimini, about 1,000 to 1,500 left the camp during the 2 years in Italy. Most of these made their way across the Alps back to Austria or Germany; others "settled" in Italy; still others were picked up by the Italian Quaestura and placed into Italian concentration camps such as Lipari, etc.

3. Of those who were successful in getting across to Austria and Germany and legalizing themselves there as DPs, a fair number have emigrated to various countries. Some are coming to the U.K. as EVWs.

4. The group of 8,500 who are now in the U.K. are the remainder of those who were most disciplined, most honourable, most loyal to their unit and to the traditions of solidarity which they had always displayed, and those who chose to follow the true, honest and legal path. They had opportunities to stay behind in Austria but they remained with the unit. Many more could have escaped from Italy but they remained loyal to British discipline. They could have been much more difficult to handle and had many opportunities and reasons for complaint, but they managed to restrain themselves and to control themselves. The fact that many oth-

162

ers of their wartime comrades have long been free and many of them resettled is well known to them and they rightly ask themselves now — does it pay to be honest and loyal and disciplined?

5. During the 2 years in Italy they were kept as "Surrendered Enemy Personnel" (SEP). This did not give them the common privileges of pay for officers, etc., allowed to prisoners of war under the Geneva Convention. On the other hand, they psychologically felt themselves a category higher than prisoner of war, not having at any time fought against the Western Allies and not having been captured as war prisoners. To a certain extent, therefore, they felt that even the classification of SEP was to some extent acknowledgment and reward for having voluntarily surrendered and for not having even taken part in any action against the Western Allies.

6. On being brought over to England in May and June of 1947, they were classified as "Prisoners of War" (POW), their date of capture being their date of arrival in the U.K. or departure from Italy. This category of classification they rightly feel has been a "lowering" of status and they wonder why?

7. The Jugoslavs who constituted a similar unit of about 12,000 were moved to the British one at the same time when the Ukrainians were moved to the U.K. a year ago. *They were all released almost immediately in the British Zone as DPs,* many of them have emigrated and are still emigrating under IRO auspices. Many are coming to U.K. as EVWs.

8. Literally thousands of Jugoslavs (ex-German forces) who "went into civilian status" on their own initiative in Italy were granted DP status, made eligible under IRO constitution and have emigrated at IRO expense. Those who could not or would not, are still in DP camps under IRO care and maintenance in Italy.

Part VI. Important Considerations.

1. These persons are not German, have never lived in Germany, have nothing in common with Germany and Germany to them is a foreign country.

2. There is no queastion of "repatriation" for after all "patria" means Motherland and their Motherland is the Province of Galicia of the Ukraine.

3. The question of the threatened deportation to Germany of those who might not prove suitable or physically fit for agriculture, (the sick, the invalids and any other similar categories,) is a very important question of PRINCIPLE. If it is accepted that persons having been employed in Great Britain are subject to be deported to a foreign country in the event

163

of their contracting an ailment, it is feared the same fate may meet all who *may* now volunteer to remain and who would prove suitable. This threat, that on the basis of a precedent the same situation may recur again, is now becoming more and more widespread among foreign workers.

4. Decisions with respect to this group of unfortunate war victims are long overdue and must be taken soon. For two years they were kept in Italy as "Surrendered Enemy Personnel" without any decision being taken. For almost a year now they have been in this country as "Prisoners of War". Those who did not go to Italy or who chose "repatriation" to Germany have since then emigrated and become resettled. The War Office has received strong instructions that all PW camps in this country must be closed as soon as possible. General public opinion is also pressing in the same direction. It is, therefore, urgent and pressing that a quick and final decision be taken with respect to the entire group in principle and with special respect to the sick, the invalided and those partially fit for employment whose future is uncertain.

5. It is known that Soviet Russia demands the REPATRIATION of all such people and especially those from Polish Ukraine, but by Russian decree they are forbidden to return to Galicia (Halychyna) which is their native land and province and which has now been annexed to Russia although it never in history belonged to Russia.

6. The high standard of education and agricultural training which is so evident among these people is largely, and perhaps entirely, due to the fact that this territory (Galicia), which was their homeland, has for over 200 years been under the influence of Vienna.

7. This group of war victims does not come within the mandate of the IRO and any of them who might be deported to Germany are not at present eligible for IRO care, maintenance and protection.

8. Should any be deported to Germany and placed into British camps, for which NO provision has been made, the British taxpayer would still be responsible for their care and maintenance.

9. If, as contemplated, some of these non-Germans are deported to Germany and handed over to the Germans, who are already overburdened with German refugees, the Germans will seek the first and every opportunity possible to get rid of them by handing them over to Soviet Poland, which in fact means Soviet Russia. Cases have been known where even sick people have been handed over to the Russians.

10. There is no need to stress and emphasize the lamentable feeling and sense of social insecurity which would spread among all the other members of the unit in question and among the foreign workers generally in

this country, if it becomes public knowledge that persons are deported for health reasons to a foreign country after having been for three years kept as prisoners of war.

11. Each and every Ukrainian worker in Great Britain, as well as all the other stronger and healthier men among the prisoners of war, together with thousands of Canadian and American citizens of Ukrainian origin, are at present disturbed concerning the future of this group of war victims.

Part VII. General Suggestions and Recommendations.

1. That immediate action should be taken to start demobilizing and discharging these men to civilian status, unconditionnally.

2. That, except for those who for security or other reasons might be considered unsuitable or unsatisfactory as settlers in this country (none are envisaged), all those who wish to accept employment in the U.K. be given the opportunity. This would save the trouble of recruiting in Germany and costs of transporting voluntary workers from Germany to this country.

3. The decision already taken that the majority should be engaged in the agricultural industry meets with general agreement and approval. Some exception must be made with regard to those who for one reason or another are unfit for agriculture but can be well utilised and employed in some other industry, such as mining, textiles, domestic, industrial (factory) work, etc.

4. That the help and co-operation of the voluntary agencies at present extending relief and welfare to Ukrainian War Victims in Western Europe should be solicited and utilised in the general civilianisation and resettlement programme and, if necessary, that they should be permitted to materially assist in the care and maintenance of those who might otherwise entirely become a charge on the country and Government.

5. That those who can make their own arrangements to immigrate to Canada or the United States or Argentine or any other country in order to join their close relatives or families, should be given every opportunity and facility to do so.

6. That the Association of Ukrainians in Great Britain, which organisation is directly and immediately responsible for their present particular welfare should be given the right and opportunity to set up a private camp or hostel, privately and independently operated, in order to assist in the care, maintenance and resettlement of the hard-core of the group, whose ultimate resettlement and employment will take a considerable time.

165

7. That such a private camp or hostel be given every necessary assistance and support from the Government authorities from the point of view of obtaining supplies, facilities, permission to place in selected employment, permission to organize private self-supporting enterprises, etc.

8. That more sympathetic consideration be given to permitting entry to the U.K. for the wives and children of those who volunteer to remain in this country as voluntary workers in the U.K.

(G.R.B. Panchuk).

218 Sussex Gardens,
Paddington,
London, W.2.

May 31st, 1948.

Selected Bibliography

Armstrong, John A. *Ukrainian Nationalism*. Reprint of 2nd ed. Little-
ton, Colorado: Ukrainian Academic Press, 1980.
Boshyk, Yury and Boris Balan. *Political Refugees and "Displaced Per-
sons," 1945-1954. A Selected Bibliography and Guide to Research
with Special Reference to Ukrainians*. The Canadian Institute of
Ukrainian Studies Research Report No. 2. 1982.
Dirks, Gerald E. *Canada's Refugee Policy: Indifference or Opportun-
ism?* Montreal: McGill-Queen's University Press, 1977.
Doroshenko, Mychajlo I. *Ukrainian Tragedy: Memoirs from World War
Two*. New York, 1980.
Elliot, Mark Rowe. *Pawns of Yalta: Soviet Refugees and America's Role
in Their Repatriation*. Urbana, Ill.: University of Illinois Press,
1982.
Frolick, Stanley W. "Saving the Displaced Persons: the Central Ukrain-
ian Relief Bureau." Speech given for the Canadian Institute of
Ukrainian Studies. Toronto, November 13, 1978.
Holborn, Louise W. *The International Refugee Organization: A Spec-
ialized Agency of the United Nations. Its History and Work, 1946-
1952*. London: Oxford University Press, 1956.
Kordan, Bohdan S. "Disunity and Duality: Ukrainian Canadians and the
Second World War." M. A. thesis, Carleton University, Ottawa,
1981.
Luciuk, Lubomyr. "The Public Record Office: An Important Source for
Archival Materials." *Journal of Ukrainian Studies* 5, no. 1. 1980.
Luciuk, Lubomyr and Zenowij Zwarycz, "The G.R.B. Panchuk Collec-
tion." *Journal of Ukrainian Studies* 7, no. 1. 1982.
Mandryka, M.I. *Ukrainian Refugees*. Winnipeg: Canadian Ukrainian
Educational Association, 1946.
Marunchak, M.H. *The Ukrainian Canadians. A History*. Winnipeg:
Ukrainian Free Academy of Sciences, 1970.
Motyl, Alexander J. *The Turn to the Right: the Ideological Origin and
Development of Ukrainian Nationalism, 1919-1929*. Boulder,
Colorado: East European Monographs, 1980.
Proudfoot, Malcolm. *European Refugees 1939-52. A Study in Forced*

167

Population Movement. London: Faber and Faber Ltd., 1957. (

Tabori, Paul. *The Anatomy of Exile. A Semantic and Historical Study*. London: Harrap, 1972.

Tarnawsky, Ostap. *Brat Bratovi/Brother's Helping Hand: History of the UUARC*. Philadelphia, 1971.

The Senate of Canada. *Proceedings of the Standing Committee on Immigration and Labour. No. 2. Wednesday, 29th May, 1946*. Ottawa: Edmound Cloutier, Printer to the King's Most Excellent Majesty, 1946.

Tolstoy, Nikolai. *Victims of Yalta*. London: Hodder and Stoughton, 1977.

Vernant, Jacques. *The Refugee in the Post-War World*. New Haven, Conn.: Yale University Press, 1953.

Woodbridge, George. *UNRRA: the History of the United Nations Relief and Rehabilitation Administration*. 3 vols. New York: Columbia University Press, 1950.

Also Available from
The Multicultural History Society of Ontario

The Italian Immigrant Woman in North America, edited by
Betty Boyd Caroli, Robert F. Harney and Lydio F. Tomasi.
1978. $7.00.

Pane e Lavoro: the Italian American Working Class, edited by
George E. Pozzetta. 1980. $8.00.

The Finnish Diaspora, edited by Michael Karni. 1981. 2 vols.
$14.00. Vol. 1: Canada, Australia, Africa, South America
and Sweden. $8.00. Vol. II: United States. $8.00.

*A Black Man's Toronto 1914-1980. The Reminiscences of Harry
Gairey*, edited by Donna Hill. 1981. $2.50.

Ukrainians in North America: a Select Bibliography, compiled
by Helena Myroniuk and Christine Worobec. 1981. $10.00.

Little Italies in North America, edited by Robert F. Harney and
J. Vincenza Scarpaci. 1981. $8.00.

The Quebec and Acadian Diaspora in North America, edited by
Raymond Breton and Pierre Savard. 1982. $8.00.

*The Gordon C. Eby Diaries, 1911-13: Chronicle of a Mennonite
Farmer*, edited and annotated by James M. Nyce. 1982.
Hardcover: $10.00, paper: $8.00.

The Polish Presence in Canada and America, edited by Frank
Renkiewicz. 1983. Hardcover: $14.00, paper: $12.00.

Dutch Immigration to North America, edited by Herman
Ganzevoort and Mark Boekelman. 1983. $9.00.

The Multicultural History Society of Ontario
43 Queen's Park Crescent East
Toronto, Ontario M5S 2C3
Canada